Scattered Light

Scattered Light

Stories by
Jean Rae Baxter

Jean Rae Baxter

Seraphim
EDITIONS

The following stories have been previously published: "Travelling by the Grand Bus Line" in *Hammered Out,* Issue 12, 2007; "The Quilt" in *A Twist of Malice,* Seraphim Editions, 2005; "An Afternoon at the Cottage" in *Ellery Queen Mystery Magazine,* December 2009; "Payback" in *Going Out With A Bang,* RendezVous Crime, 2008; "Osprey Lake" in *Indian Country Noir,* Akashic Books, 2010. An earlier version of "After Annabelle" was published as "Hole in One" in *Hammered Out,* Issue 12, 2007.

The publisher gratefully acknowledges the financial assistance of the Canada Council for the Arts.

Canada Council   Conseil des Arts
for the Arts   du Canada

Library and Archives Canada Cataloguing in Publication

Baxter, Jean Rae
    Scattered light : stories / by Jean Rae Baxter.

ISBN 978-0-9808879-9-0

    I. Title.

PS8603.A935S33 2011   C813'.6   C2011-905099-4

Editor: George Down
Author Photo: Today's Faces Photography
Cover Design and Typography: Julie McNeill, McNeill Design Arts

Published in 2011 by
Seraphim Editions
54 Bay Street
Woodstock, ON
Canada N4S 3K9

Printed and bound in Canada

In Memory of

Kerry Schooley

Mentor, editor, and friend

Contents

After Annabelle

The bones slept while I grew. They were my cousin Annabelle's bones. I spent the first decade of my life in the shadow of her disappearance. A shadow cast by absence. The darkest kind.

While the bones slept, my secret grew. One good wind would topple the old maple tree, spill what was hidden in its dead heart's hollow core. I've been waiting thirty years for that wind.

I never knew Annabelle. She vanished the summer I was born, vanished while hunting golf balls in the rough at Hidden Valley Golf Club. As a child, I heard the story a thousand times.

The kids who had gone ball hunting with Annabelle returned to Kilbride without her. They weren't worried about her – not at first. Annabelle must have been hiding on them, they thought, because she did things like that to get attention. Once she pretended her ankle was broken, so two boys had to make a chair with their hands linked to carry her half a mile through the woods. They were mad when it turned out her ankle was fine. So when Annabelle disappeared, they thought it would serve her right if they left for home without her.

My Uncle Hugh and Aunt Rita didn't suspect anything was wrong until Annabelle didn't show up for supper. They supposed she was playing at one of the other kids' houses.

But after they phoned around and nobody had seen her since four in the afternoon, they started to fret. By eight o'clock, when it began to get dark, they were frantic. Uncle Hugh rounded up half a dozen neighbours and he brought along Susie, his yellow Labrador retriever – not good at following a scent, he always said, but eager as they come.

After they had looked for an hour without finding any trace of Annabelle, Uncle Hugh called the police. The next morning a real search began, with trained dogs, tracking experts, and dozens of volunteers.

Annabelle's picture and description appeared in newspapers and on TV. Missing-person posters all over Ontario asked if anybody had seen Annabelle Jenking. Age: Ten. Height: Four feet, six inches. Copper-red curls, blue eyes, freckles. Last seen wearing a white T-shirt, blue shorts, blue ankle socks and white sneakers,

For three days, the searchers were out from dawn to dark. Then the search was called off. My dad had been out with the searchers every day. When he got home on the last day of the search, he sank into his chair, muddy boots on the carpet, and stared for a long time at one-month-old me, Nora Jenking, blanket-wrapped in Mom's arms. Finally he said, "No daughter of mine is ever going to earn pocket money looking for golf balls."

"Never," my mother had agreed, visualizing the shadowy form of a tramp slipping through the trees, a dirty hand clamped over Annabelle's mouth, strong arms dragging her through the bushes. The act that followed was more than she could bear to imagine. The terror. The blood. The limp body borne away.

No trace of Annabelle ever turned up. Every lead turned out to be false. After ten years there was still no body, no suspect, and no idea of what had happened.

Aunt Rita and Uncle Hugh never got over their loss. Every year on Annabelle's birthday, Aunt Rita brought out her big scrapbook and made me look at Annabelle's baptismal certificate and her report cards, all the birthday cards she had ever received, and dozens of snapshots. Sometimes I caught Aunt Rita staring at me and then turning her face away. Once I asked Mom why my aunt looked at me funny.

"Because you look like Annabelle," my mother said.

This was true. The framed photograph of Annabelle on Uncle Hugh and Aunt Rita's piano could have fooled even me.

One day, when I was about nine, I overheard my parents and my aunt and uncle talking about Annabelle.

"I want closure," Aunt Rita said. "Until I know for sure that she's dead, I can't move on."

The way it sounded, she *hoped* somebody would find Annabelle's body. This was weird.

As long as Annabelle's body was not found, I could keep on dreaming that she would show up alive some day. I pictured her driving into Kilbride in a shiny red convertible, stopping in front of her parents' house, getting out of her car. She would be about eighteen years old. Tall and gorgeous, with copper curls tumbling to her shoulders, and blue eyes just like mine. As long as nobody found her body, I believed this could happen.

Uncle Hugh and Aunt Rita's wish for closure made no sense to me. Nor did my parents' rule, *"Thou shalt not hunt for golf balls,"* which was the First Commandment in their book.

By the time I was ten, all my friends were earning money from selling golf balls they'd found in the rough, scrubbed and presented neatly in egg cartons. Four dollars a dozen.

The marketplace was the lawn behind the Hidden Valley clubhouse. Sales started just after eleven every Sunday morning, when Sunday school was out and the early golfers had finished their round. The kids would meet the golfers on their way from the eighteenth hole to the clubhouse. Business was brisk.

The club members counted on the village children to supply gently-used golf balls at a bargain price. The kids counted on the members for pocket money.

I considered it unfair to be shut out of the golf-ball business because of something that had happened when I was just a baby. Burning with envy, I watched my friends return muddy, mosquito-bitten and victorious from each ball-hunting expedition. They told me that golf-ball hunting was as much fun as fishing – which my parents didn't object to, but I hated. Every time I tried to put a worm on a hook, I felt the poor worm's suffering. Besides, the golf-ball hunter had a better chance of success than the fisherman because a ball, once spotted, never got away.

And the rewards! Instead of a slimy fish that had to be scaled and cleaned, there was cash to spend at the Kilbride General Store on licorice pipes, gumballs, candy cigarettes, and comic books.

So I rebelled.

"This summer, I'm going to hunt golf balls," I told my best friend, Barbara.

It was a Saturday afternoon in June. We were sitting on the edge of the wide porch in front of the Kilbride General Store, sharing a box of Reese's Pieces that Barbara had paid for.

"But your parents won't let you."

"They won't find out. I'll go by myself when there's nobody else around. You'll be the only person who knows about it, and I trust you not to tell on me. If you sell the balls I find, I'll pay you one dollar for every four dollars you get."

Barbara popped another Reese's Piece into her mouth. As she chewed, I could almost hear her mind working.

"Who'll wash your golf balls and pack them in egg cartons?"

"You, I guess. I can't take them to my house."

"If I have to wash them, pack them, and sell them, I want two dollars."

Go halvers! That was high. But she had a point.

"Oh, all right."

A handful of Reese's Pieces sealed the deal. As I munched, I felt a big bubble of happiness swell inside. No more mooching. Soon I'd have money to buy my own treats.

"When are you going to start?" Barbara asked.

"Tomorrow."

"What about Sunday school?"

"Sunday school makes it the perfect time. I'll have more than an hour while you're all at Sunday school. Afterwards, maybe you can give me your Sunday school handout to show my parents."

"I guess so." She scratched the dirt with the toe of her running shoe. "You'll wreck your good clothes in the rough. You need to wear old clothes."

"I've thought about that. This afternoon I'll put some old clothes in a plastic bag and hide it in that culvert on the Cumminsville Road."

"Sounds like a plan." Barbara stood up. "Gotta go home. Chores."

Dad and Uncle Hugh were having a beer on the front porch when I reached home. Just looking at them, you'd know they were brothers. They had the same coppery hair and blue eyes. Uncle Hugh's eyes were sadder than Dad's, and he had more creases in his forehead.

"Nora, any chance you've seen Susie?" my uncle asked as I climbed the steps.

"Nope." I opened the screen door.

"She's been missing since yesterday."

"Gee. That's too bad." I stopped without going inside and stood there not knowing what to say. Uncle Hugh and his old yellow Lab went everywhere together, Susie keeping close to his heels. She always sat beside him on the passenger seat when he delivered the rural mail.

"Susie will come home," my dad said. "She's too old to steal and too smart to get run over."

"A fourteen-year-old dog doesn't run off," said Uncle Hugh.

Although I loved Susie, I agreed with Dad that nobody would steal her. Susie smelled bad, especially her breath. It stank like rotten meat. In dog years, she was ninety-eight.

"If I see Susie, I'll bring her back."

I went inside the house. In my closet I found pants and a shirt I had outgrown but could still squeeze into, as well as a pair of sneakers with holes in the toes. Then I snitched a length of red yarn from Mom's knitting basket. This was to mark the hiding place where I would leave my ball-hunting clothes between expeditions. When I had stuffed everything into a plastic bag, I went out the back door so nobody would see me. The culvert on the Cumminsville Road was just outside Kilbride, on the way to Hidden Valley. I climbed down into the ditch and shoved my bag into the culvert as far as I could reach.

In the morning I headed off early to avoid the kids who really were going to Sunday school. After retrieving my bag of old clothes from the culvert, I took a shortcut through the woods.

That was when things started to go wrong. As soon as the blackflies saw me coming, they descended in a cloud. I was slapping and slapping at them, feeling mad at myself for not thinking to bring a little jar of bug spray.

I changed into my old clothes before climbing the fence at the rear of the golf course property. Then I folded my Sunday school clothes and hid them under a big burdock leaf. The blackflies were at me every minute, and then an army of mosquitoes joined the attack.

According to the other kids, the rough beside the first fairway, on the east side, was the best location for ball hunting. It was part marsh and part woods, the soggy parts thick with tall grasses that looked like bamboo, and the dry parts covered with trees, bracken fern and tiger lilies.

The spot where I began searching was a few feet off the fairway, behind a curtain of cedar trees. I found three balls in the first ten minutes.

Golfers were already on the course. I could see them, but they couldn't see me. One pair hopped out of their golf cart not twenty feet from where I stood. I heard the whip of a club, but no whack.

"Shit!" the golfer said.

"Call it a mulligan." The other golfer swung his club. This time the whipping sound ended with a solid crack.

The man who'd spoken first said, "Good distance."

"Yeah. I had my balls irradiated. You should try it. Ten percent increased length."

A laugh. "That must help your sex life too."

They climbed into the golf cart, and it rolled up the slope in the direction of the green.

In the distance, church bells were ringing. The clang of the United Church bell in Kilbride made a nice harmony with the bong of the Anglican bell a mile to the east. Ding-dong. Dinga-ding-dong. Usually I liked the sound of the bells. But this time they made me feel guilty. What was I doing, sneaking away when I was supposed to be in Sunday school?

I wished that I were back in Kilbride, in the dim church basement, learning about the Light of the World. Maybe God had sent those blackflies and mosquitoes to punish me for skipping – like plagues of locusts in the Old Testament.

But I was determined not to quit until I had a dozen balls.

As I worked my way from the drier to the soggier ground, I found another half-dozen. My pockets bulged. Three more would be enough.

At the edge of a shallow stream I sat on a log to rub my bites with mud. That took away some of the itch, and I was starting to feel more cheerful when I spotted a snapping turtle the size of a meat platter sunning itself six feet away. It had green moss in the ridges of its shell, and beady eyes that fixed on me. I wriggled sideways to put more space between us. The turtle stretched out its long, skinny neck so far you'd think it was about to climb out of its shell. I'd never heard of anyone being charged by a turtle, but there's always a first time.

I picked up a stick the size of a cane. The stick might be useful for fighting off turtles, I thought, or for dividing the grass as I searched for balls.

I was heading for higher ground when I saw the bluebottle flies. There were thousands, buzzing around one particular spot in the undergrowth, hovering over it in a dancing swarm. They must have found the carcass of something big. I took one step closer. Then another.

Now I could see it. Under an undulating carpet of bluebottle flies lay the shape of a dog. I struck with my stick. The cloud of flies lifted. I saw the body of a yellow Labrador. The flies settled again.

"Susie!" A sob choked my throat.

I just wanted to go home, and it was time to leave anyway. I found three more balls as I worked my way toward the rear fence. Now I had a dozen. Four dollars was big money, even if I had to split it with Barbara.

There were big maple trees near the fence. One appeared to be hollow, with an opening at its base between two thick roots that stretched over the ground. I thrust my stick into the opening. The stick went way, way in. Just the sort of hole I needed to hide my old clothes for next time – if there was a next time. I got down on my hands and knees to look inside. No beady eyes peered out at me. I reached my hand into the hollow space. Sawdust, cool and crumbly. There must be termites in the tree. My fingers closed on something hard and smooth. I pulled out a bone about as long as my thigh. I was scared, but curious too. I reached into the hole again. Another bone. Then a child's sneaker, with shreds of fabric that had once been white. And a blue sock.

That's when I stopped.

Back into the hole went the bones and the sneaker and the sock. Then I changed into my Sunday school clothes and shoved my old clothes into the hole. I put the balls I had found into the plastic bag.

On my way to Barbara's house I was shaking so hard I could hardly walk. I stopped at the horse trough outside the General Store. With my hanky dipped in water, I wiped the mud and blood from my legs, arms, neck and face.

Barbara was watching out the window for me. She met me at her front door before I had time to knock.

"You look awful," she said as she took the bag of golf balls from me. "Your face is lumpy and you're covered with bites. Next time, remember to take bug spray with you."

"There won't be a next time. Golf-ball hunting is not for me."

She tilted her head, inspecting me. "Maybe you're right. Sooner or later your parents would find out, anyway."

The ice cream and candy that I bought with my share of the golf ball money didn't taste as good as they should have.

Pretty soon Uncle Hugh figured out for himself that old Susie had wandered off to die. I'm glad he never knew about the bluebottle flies.

Uncle Hugh and Aunt Rita died a few years ago, without closure. My parents passed away soon after.

Chelsea, my youngest child, is eleven years old. She has copper-red curls, blue eyes and freckles. She hunts golf balls with the other kids. Business is brisk Sunday mornings on the lawn behind the Hidden Valley clubhouse. Chelsea rolls her eyes when I warn her never to go into the woods by herself.

I'm still waiting for the wind that will topple that maple tree, bring everything to light. And yet there's no one left who cares.

Osprey Lake

"Keep the engine running," Don said.

Heather turned off the headlights. By the street lamp's bluish light she could still see his narrow, impassive face and the dark eyes that looked right through her. With his parka hood up and the cord pulled tight, he didn't need a mask.

She wanted to say something, open her mouth at least. But she couldn't. She just sat there, gloved hands on the wheel, wishing she'd had the guts to refuse when Kevin told her that she had to go with Don, that she would be the driver.

Don fiddled with the door handle. "You're scared shitless, aren't you?"

"I'm okay."

When he left the car, she leaned back, knowing that she couldn't escape now. There was no escape.

A car passed, then a taxi. Not much traffic. The cold kept people indoors. At 11:30 p.m. Maitland Street was a dead zone, with only the Hasti Mart still open.

In the side mirror she saw Don, swinging the empty gym bag, walk past the Dark Side Tattoo Studio and the Ritz Tanning Salon, then pull open the Hasti Mart's door. She knew the plan. He'd show the Paki his gun. Maybe not a real gun, but it looked real. In one minute Don would be out of there, with the gym bag full of smokes and the money from the till.

"I don't want to be the driver," she had told Kevin.

"I wouldn't ask you if the boss hadn't called me in."

"Why not wait till the next time you're off work? The Hasti Mart isn't going anywhere."

"This has to be tonight."

"I don't see why."

"You don't need to know."

She sat there with her eyes closed, trying not to think about Kevin. But he was all she ever thought about, his handsome face plastered inside her eyelids like one of those ads for electric shavers, with an adoring woman stroking his manly cheeks.

Kevin knew she didn't like Don. When she told him, he just shrugged. Kevin had a habit of shrugging whenever she spoke her mind. If he had to choose between them, he'd choose Don. "We been through a lot together," he'd said. "A lot of what?" "Stuff."

When she opened her eyes, she saw Don in the side mirror sprinting toward the car, leaning slightly from the weight of the gym bag. He opened the door, jumped in, turned his face toward her. His blood-splattered face.

"Get moving!"

She pulled away from the curb before he had the door closed.

"Are you hurt? There's blood on your face."

"Not my blood."

"What happened?"

"Don't ask. Just drive."

Her mouth opened and closed again. Dread swallowed all her words.

"Get onto the 401."

"Where we going?"

"North. Up the 400. I know a place."

"We got to tell Kevin. What'll he think when we don't bring back his car?"

"He'll know."

She felt a void open in front of her and clutched the wheel, fighting not to fall in. "Is the Paki dead?"

"Damn fool came at me with a tire iron. I got it away from him. Yeah, he's dead."

Don threw off his parka hood, reached in the glove compartment for a pack of cigarettes, lit one. His eyes were fixed on the road, and his face was a blank.

He didn't snap out of it until they were almost to Barrie.

"Take the Highway 11 exit," he said.

"Highway 11. Muskoka?"

"More or less."

"Maybe you could tell me where we're going?"

"Osprey Lake."

"Never heard of it."

"There's a cottage where we can hide while I figure out what to do."

"Not me," she said. "You can drive there by yourself. I'll split when we get to Barrie and take the bus back to Toronto."

"You crazy? How do I know you won't call the cops?" Don lit another cigarette. His hands shook.

"I don't want trouble," she said. "I won't tell anybody but Kevin. Not ever. I'll just go home."

"The hell you will."

From the corner of her eye she saw the gun pointing at her.

"That's not real," she said. "Kevin told me."

"You shouldn't believe everything Kevin says."

"I didn't hear a shot, back at the Hasti Mart."

"I used his tire iron."

Until they were fifty kilometres past Barrie, he kept the gun on her. She didn't believe it was real. But how would she know? She had never touched a gun in all her life, not even seen one up close. Maybe Kevin had lied.

To him, holdups were 'Trick or Treat', a game to play when you outgrew Halloween. Kevin was twenty-five, cashier at a self-serve gas station. He'd worked there for six years. Just temporary. As soon as he got a break, he'd be big-time.

A frosty halo circled the moon. It was going to snow. Eight inches by morning, according to the six o'clock forecast. Heather hoped it would hold off until they got wherever they were going. So far, the roads were bare.

"Turn right at the crossroads," Don said.

She touched the brake. At the corner, signs nailed to a tall post pointed toward cottages east, west and straight ahead. Some signs were too faded to read, but on others Heather could make out the lettering: Brad & Judy Smith, The MacTeers, Bide-a-wee, The Pitts, and a dozen more.

"Are we going to one of those?"

"No. There used to be a sign. It fell off years ago. But I know the way."

The ruts were four inches deep. No gravel. Just frozen mud as hard as granite. Driving on railroad tracks might be like this if you had to stay on top of the rails. But railway tracks ran straight, and these ruts veered wherever a boulder or a big tree had stood in the path of whoever cleared this track. Wilderness crowded the road. The bare twig ends of birch and maple trees and the swishing boughs of spruce, fir and balsam brushed the car's sides.

Wooden arrows nailed to tree trunks pointed to the turnoffs to individual cottages. These turnoffs, the only spots where a car could turn around if it had to, were few and far between.

The track was getting worse. Heather leaned forward, high beams on, studying the ruts. "Are we nearly there?"

Don's lighter flared. "Ten minutes."

"There hasn't been a turnoff for half a kilometre."

"That's right. We've passed Mud Fish Lake. That's as far as they've brought the hydro. Osprey Lake is next."

"Who lives there?"

"There used to be Ojibwas, but they got cleared out years ago. Now it's just a few cottagers in summer. People who like it wild."

"What about winter?"

"There's sort of a village at the far end of Osprey Lake. Maybe eight houses."

The car jolted in and out of the ruts. Was it better to drive in the ruts or to try to stay on top of the rims? I should have stopped outside Barrie, Heather thought, called his bluff. But at least there's a village on Osprey Lake. Sort of a village.

"What do people do in that village?"

"They mind their own business. Why don't you?"

She pulled the wheel to the right to miss a rock outcrop twenty feet high. In front of the car, a tree with a two-foot-diameter trunk lay across the track. Heather braked hard.

"Shit!" Don said, opening the car door.

"What now?"

"We walk."

"How far?"

"About one kilometre." He picked up the gym bag.

She wasn't dressed for this. Jeans, a leather bomber jacket, and pant boots with three-inch heels. Walking bent over, hugging herself for warmth, she tripped over a frozen rut, struggled to her feet, took one step and stumbled sideways. "Oh, shit!" The heel of one boot had snapped off. On her knees she fumbled in the dark until she found the heel. Shoving it into her pocket, she lurched after Don.

He left the track and headed into the bush. She could not see a path, but he seemed to know his way.

The cottage's tall windows were what she saw first, a dull gleam of glass facing the lake. Trees and shadow obscured the rest of the cottage. Behind it rose a wooded hill.

"Here we are," Don said.

"How do we get in?"

"There's a key."

He crouched at the threshold, reached under a board, and rose with a key in his hand. He paused, staring at the key as if it held a great mystery, before inserting it into the lock. The door stuck until he hurled his weight against it. Don stepped inside and motioned her to follow.

"It's colder in here than it was outside." She took a step, bumped into something that felt like a chair.

"It feels colder because you expect it to be warmer."

Don set down the gym bag and pulled out his lighter. Its brief flare revealed a massive stone fireplace. He stepped across the room, lit a candle that stood on the mantel.

The room came more clearly into view. Open rafters. Walls panelled with wide boards. Pictures on the walls. A plank table and half a dozen wooden chairs. A cluster of tubular furniture with loose cushions: three chairs and one loveseat.

This was better than she had expected. It wasn't a shack.

He too was looking around. "Hasn't changed."

"Since when?"

"Eight years. The last time I was here."

"Who owns it?"

"My grandfather's estate."

So that was the connection. Don Carson, petty crook, had summered here as a child. A loser like Don. It didn't fit.

"This way," he said. She hobbled after him into a room at the back. He closed the door. "If we stay here in the bedroom, nobody out on the ice can see a light."

"Who's out there to see anything?"

"You never can tell."

"At four in the morning when it's ten below?"

A squall of wind rattled the windows.

She looked around the room. There was a double bed with an iron bedstead, an old-fashioned dresser, and an open closet with wire hangers on a rod.

He set the candlestick on the dresser. Pulling two sleeping bags from the closet shelf, he thrust one at her. The fabric was riddled with tiny holes. Even cold, it smelled of mouse.

"Where do we sleep?" she asked.

"There." He pointed to the bed.

"Both of us?"

"Unless you prefer the floor."

"You mean there's only one bed in the whole cottage?"

"There used to be two bunkhouses for sleeping, until their roofs fell in."

If she had to choose between the bed and the floor, she'd take the bed. She wasn't worried about Don bothering her – his best friend's girl. Heather wasn't sure he liked women anyway.

He unrolled his sleeping bag. Heather made no move.

"I need to go to the bathroom," she said.

"Bathroom!" he snorted. "There's an outhouse, if it hasn't fallen down."

"Where … if it's still there?"

"Up the hill. I'll show you."

She limped after him back to the main room

"Did you twist your ankle?"

"The heel broke off one of my boots."

"Huh!" He started to laugh, and then seemed to change his mind.

To the right of the fireplace there was a door in the back wall. Don pulled the bolt. "Straight up the path. You might find an old phone book if you need paper."

Through the darkness Heather saw a shed about a hundred feet up the hill. That must be it. She scrambled up the path on her hands and knees. When she reached the outhouse and pulled on the latch, the door fell off, knocking her backwards.

"Damn!" She pushed the door off and hauled herself to her feet.

No time to be squeamish. Heather pulled down her jeans and panties and lowered her bottom over the hole in the board seat. Gasping at the blast of frigid air, she imagined monsters with icy fingers reaching up from the dark lagoon.

When she returned, Don was sitting on the side of the bed, smoking.

"How do you like our outhouse?"

"The door fell off and knocked me over."

"That's our ghost. When I was a young kid, I thought the outhouse was haunted. I hated going there at night."

"I never heard of a haunted outhouse before."

"Family secret. When my grandfather dug the pit, he uncovered a skull and a bunch of bones. Old Indian grave. There were arrowheads and shells and a stone pipe."

She shuddered. "Under the outhouse?"

"It wasn't an outhouse then."

"All the same, he should have put it someplace else."

"Anywhere on that hillside would be the same. You have to move an outhouse every few years and dig a new pit. Every pit they dug, they found another grave." He tossed his cigarette on the floor and ground it out with his boot. "An old Indian told my grandfather that this was sacred land. He said we ought to respect the ancestors buried here."

"Maybe you should."

"It's just superstition."

"Hey! Let's not talk about graveyards. It spooks me out."

Heather kicked off her boots, unrolled her sleeping bag and crawled in. She couldn't stop shivering until her body heat had warmed the narrow space. That was when the smell took over. Mouse dirt and mould. Her throat tickled and her breath wheezed.

Don went outside, but not for long enough to go up to the outhouse. When he returned, he pinched out the candle and lay down with his back to her.

The mattress sagged, with a dip in the middle. Heather had to hold on to the edge to keep from rolling into the hollow. But some time during the night, gravity won. Her grip on the mattress loosened, and she awoke to feel Don's body against hers. The warmth was welcome.

The mattress creaked. Heather half opened her eyes. It was morning. Don, still in his sleeping bag, had swung his legs around so that he was sitting on the edge of the bed. He lit a cigarette.

"Are you awake?"

"Uh-huh."

"Look out the window."

Rising on one elbow, she looked through the dirty glass.

Snow filled the air with feathery clumps. The forecast had been right. The snow would already be over the tops of her pant boots, and it was still falling. Even if one heel weren't broken, she couldn't walk far in that.

Don unzipped his sleeping bag and stood up. "Do you know how to light a Coleman?"

"A what?"

"Jeez! Don't you know anything? It's a kerosene stove. For cooking."

"You mean there's food around here?"

"Look in the kitchen."

"Where's the kitchen?"

"Since this cottage only has four rooms, you should be able to find it."

She unzipped her sleeping bag and crawled past him. Christ, it was cold! With the sleeping bag draped over her shoulders, she tottered into the main room. The gym bag was no longer where Don had set it down.

Daylight brought to life the pictures hanging on the board walls. Some were the usual Canadiana: water, rocks and trees. Others were blown-up snapshots of people having fun. A laughing girl in a canoe. A raccoon accepting food from a woman's outstretched hand. A boy holding up a string of fish. She took a second look at the boy. He was skinny, with a narrow face. He might have been Don at twelve or thirteen.

He came up behind her as she studied the picture. "Is that you?" she asked.

"Kid brother."

"I never heard you mention him."

"He's dead."

"Oh. Sorry."

"C'mon. Let's get some breakfast."

The kitchen was at the front of the cottage: a narrow room with a door at the far end and a window overlooking the lake. Under the window was a chipped enamelled sink, with a rusty hand pump mounted beside it on the counter. Next to that stood a metal object that looked like a hotplate on a stand with an upside-down glass jug, half-filled with a clear yellowish liquid, suspended underneath.

"That's the Coleman," Don said. "It's fifty years old, but it works." He fiddled with a knob and flicked his lighter. A ring of blue flames spurted.

"It smells funny."

"Kerosene. You'll get used to it."

"Okay. Show me the food."

He pointed to a row of large, dusty jars labelled with masking tape, all empty except for "Sugar", "Rice", "Flour", and "Macaroni".

"That's it." He picked up a pail. "I'm going outside to get snow we can melt for water."

"Doesn't the pump work?"

"Jeez!" he said. "At ten below?"

Heather boiled rice for breakfast. With sugar added, it was edible. Don smoked right through the meal.

After eating, he brought in logs from the woodpile outside the back door and lit a fire in the fireplace. Heather, huddled in the loveseat with the sleeping bag over her legs, stretched out her hands to the warmth.

"Enjoy it while you can," he said. "As soon as the snow stops, I'll have to put out the fire. Smoke from the chimney is a dead giveaway somebody's here." He dragged a chair to the fire and settled himself.

Heather looked around at her surroundings. Daylight revealed years of neglect. The dark green seat cushions were stained. Dirty white stuffing bulged from their burst seams. Dust covered everything.

"Doesn't anybody ever come here?" she asked

"Not any more."

"Why not?"

"There was an accident." He paused. "Sooner or later the place will be sold. My dad and my uncle are suing each other over the estate. Both their lawyers told them to stay away." His lank hair fell across his eyes, and he pushed it back irritably. He hated questions. But if she didn't ask, how would she find out anything?

"What are you going to do about the car?"

"Nothing, right now."

"You can't just leave it there. It's covered with DNA."

The Paki's DNA in the front seat, Heather's and Kevin's in the back. They'd had sex in the Mustang dozens of times. Hair. Semen. The police could make plenty out of that.

"Here's what's going to happen," Don said. "Kevin will report his car stolen. Nothing for him to worry about. His alibi is watertight."

"What about us? We don't have alibis. And we can't stay here forever."

"I'll figure out something."

She suspected that Don didn't have a clue what to do next. What did he face if he got caught? Life? Twenty-five years? That was his problem. She wasn't the one who'd killed the Paki. Her smart move would be to turn herself in. Co-operate in return for a reduced sentence. But that would drag Kevin into it and she couldn't do that.

All this trouble for the sake of a few lousy dollars.

It snowed all day. Heather sat in front of the fire with a book open on her lap. *Curtain: Poirot's Last Case.* There were plenty of those old Agatha Christie mysteries lying around the cottage. She wished she had something different to read. A romance might take her mind off her problems. She never did like crime stories. Especially not now.

Don fell asleep, dozing in his chair with his skinny legs stretched toward the fire.

This would be a good time to do something about her boots. Closing the cover on Monsieur Poirot, she pulled the broken heel from her pocket. It looked simple: just slices of leather stacked and glued to form a column. All she needed was a knife to make the two heels match. She stood up, wincing when her feet met the cold floor, and carried her boots into the kitchen.

Don sighed, shifted in his chair.

Rummaging through a drawer full of assorted cutlery, she found a fish-scaling knife with a sawtooth blade. The knife squeaked as it chewed through the leather of the unbroken heel.

She was half finished when Don came up behind her.

"What are you doing?" His fingers squeezed her wrist so tightly she dropped the knife.

"Fixing my boots."

"You don't need them. You aren't going anywhere."

He snatched the boot she was working on, picked up the other from the countertop, and strode into the main room. Without another word, he hurled them into the fire.

"No!" she yelled.

Don grabbed her before she could reach the fireplace tongs. He held her by both shoulders to watch the tongues of blue and green flames lick the leather of her boots. The soles peeled away from the vamps, and the heels sweated beads of glue. Don did not loosen his grip until two charred lumps were all that remained.

The next morning, sunshine sparkled on the lake. Around the cottage, evergreen boughs bent under their burden of snow.

They ate boiled macaroni. Don put out the fire.

"We're going to freeze." Heather said.

"The fireplace will hold heat for a couple of days."

"And then what?"

"I told you, I'll figure something out."

"You better hurry. We'll run out of food in three or four days." Freeze or starve, she thought. What difference did it make?

She padded across the cold floor to the windows. Now that the snow had stopped, she could see clear across the lake. Off to her left was the village, smoke rising from snow-covered roofs. Straight ahead was a tiny island. The only tree on the island was a dead pine missing half its branches. A rough platform of sticks balanced on the top, capped with snow.

"What's that thing on the dead tree?"

He looked up without moving from his chair. "Osprey nest."

"You're kidding."

"Why should I be kidding? This is Osprey Lake. Ospreys live here."

"It doesn't look like they live here now."

"They fly south for the winter."

"They're not so dumb. At least they're smarter than the people in those houses. I wonder what they do all winter long, stuck in the snow?"

"They get around on their snowmobiles. When they aren't drinking, they tend their traplines. Most are fishing guides in summer and trappers in the winter. Except for Rosemary Bear Paw. She's a bootlegger."

"Indian?"

"Ojibwa, like the rest of them living over there. Anishinabe is what they call themselves. It means Real People. It was her old man who warned my grandfather about the ancestors' graves. Rosemary is the guardian of some sacred scrolls. She belongs to a religious society."

"You said she was a bootlegger."

"It's not like she's a nun. When we were kids, Rosemary supplied us with smokes and liquor. She thought that was funny, a native selling liquor to whites."

"Man bites dog."

"You can put it that way. Sometimes we paid for liquor with things we found in the graves. Stuff they buried with their dead."

"What sort of things?"

"Arrowheads. Pipe bowls. Different things. There may still be some in the junk room. Want to see it?"

"As long as there aren't any bones."

"Naw. We threw the bones we found into the pit to get rid of them."

The junk room was on the far side of the kitchen door. Heather watched from the doorway as Don picked his way through a jumble of fishing poles, paddles, life jackets and broken cartons. She saw a can labelled "kerosene", and a single rubber boot.

"I found it." Don lifted a rusty tackle box from under a heap of junk. Heather followed him back to the main room, where a bit of heat still radiated from the fireplace stones.

He opened the latches of the tackle box. "Have a look."

Cautiously she peered inside. The first thing she picked up was a stone pipe bowl carved with the image of a bear.

"Cool," Heather said. "Does it, like, mean anything?"

"The bear would be the guy's manitou – his guardian spirit."

Next she picked up an object that looked like a knife blade, although it was corroded and green.

"That's a copper knife," Don said.

"I didn't know there was copper around here."

"There isn't. The Ojibwa did a lot of trading. You'll find copper arrowheads, too. And cowrie shells from the ocean."

A second pipe bowl was carved with the image of a crane. There were dozens of beads, both glass and shell. Heather picked up a small clay bowl that had a lopsided, frowning face etched into its side.

"You know what?" she said. "You could sell this stuff on eBay."

"Not a bad idea." Don lit a cigarette. "Maybe we'll take it with us."

"If we ever get out of here."

"Don't start on that again."

Don shovelled everything back into the tackle box. His jaw clenched.

He has no plan, she thought. Without Kevin to tell him, he doesn't know what to do.

The sudden thought of Kevin filled her with desperate longing. She had not seen him for two whole days.

Heather could not believe her luck that Kevin had chosen her out of all the girls he might have had. Flat-chested with a big butt, she wasn't much to look at. But Kevin was gorgeous – movie star handsome. Great mop of gold-brown hair. Dreamy grey eyes. And that amazing smile!

It had been a warm July day when Kevin first came into the drugstore where she worked. He had bought toothpaste. She remembered that because of his smile – the kind of smile that sells toothpaste on TV. Their fingers brushed when she handed him his change.

Next day he was back to buy condoms. When she saw what they were, blood rushed to her face and she could not meet his eyes.

"When are you done working?" he had asked.

She didn't answer. But at four o'clock, the end of her shift, her heart beat fast to see him leaning against a black Mustang in the drugstore parking lot. He wore tight jeans and a black shirt open at the neck.

"Can I give you a lift?"

"No thanks. I don't have far to walk."

He had smiled. "We can go for a drive." Something shivered in the air between them. "My name's Kevin."

"I'm Heather."

"I know."

"How?"

"Your badge."

"Oh." She had felt her cheeks redden.

I shouldn't be doing this, she had thought as she climbed into the passenger seat. From the beginning, she couldn't say no to Kevin.

He drove fast, with the window open and one arm along the back of the passenger seat. They had stopped for a hamburger at a crossroads restaurant, and then kept on going. He had parked his car down by a river just past a little town. It was very quiet, almost as if the town were miles away, not barely out of sight behind a hill.

He had a green plaid blanket in the trunk. Heather, pretending she didn't know what was coming, wished that she were wearing sexy underwear instead of cotton briefs. As he pulled her down onto the blanket, she remembered the condoms. Kevin was prepared. He took a lot for granted, didn't he?

With her next paycheque, Heather had purchased five pairs of lace panties at La Senza. For the rest of the summer, she and Kevin made love a couple of times a week, either on the plaid blanket or in the back seat – depending on the weather. In November, when it got cold, he had started taking her home. That was when she met Don. Within a month, she moved in with them.

To help out with expenses, Heather had stolen things from the drugstore: condoms, toothpaste, aftershave. It was easy.

Everything was perfect until the day Kevin said, "I've figured out a way to make some real money."

"How?"

"There's stuff with street value in that drugstore. Uppers. Downers. Dexedrine. Cold remedies. We can make crystal meth out of cold remedies right here in the kitchen." His eyes had locked on hers. "What about it?"

She had felt scared. "I can't. I don't have access to the dispensary."

"I don't see any bars keeping you out."

"Only the pharmacists ever go behind that counter."

"Come on, Heather. Don't tell me you can't." A deep sigh. "This is the first thing I ever asked you to do."

Although that wasn't true, she had allowed it to pass. Kevin had pushed her for a couple of weeks before giving up. A cloud settled over their relationship. She had let him down.

Would she still be his girlfriend if she let him down again? Did she have to steal things to keep him? Was that the price? But what could she do? If she lost Kevin, she'd just about die.

Mr. Stonefield, the drugstore owner, had caught her sneaking a bottle of aftershave into her purse and fired her on the spot. Peering at her through the middle section of his trifocals, he said she was lucky he didn't lay charges. This was true. But now she had no job, no income, and no chance to pick up little extras for Kevin. Again, she had let him down. Another reason she could not have refused to drive that night.

The next day while Don napped – all he ever did was smoke and sleep – Heather had a bright idea. The rubber boot she had noticed in the junk room must have a mate. She tiptoed to the junk room. And there she found it, buried under some rotted canvas. When she turned the boot upside down, mouse dirt and popcorn kernels rained onto the floor.

They were men's boots. Each had the number 13 embossed in its red sole. Gingerly she pulled them on and took a few steps. It was like trying to walk with her feet in a pair of cardboard cartons. This was not going to work unless she could make her feet larger to fill the space. An old shirt lay amidst the junk. She tore it into strips, which she wrapped like a big, bulky bandage around each foot.

Don opened his eyes as she stomped into the main room.

"You look like a circus clown," he said.

"I don't care what I look like. My feet were so cold they hurt."

For the rest of the day she clomped around, bumping into furniture and tripping over her own feet so he would see that she couldn't possibly escape with those on her feet. He let her keep the rubber boots.

Blame the cold. Blame the mattress. It wasn't Heather's fault that their bodies rolled together in the middle of the night. She was half asleep when she felt his penis, hard and thick, right through two layers of insulated fabric, against her thigh. A ripple of desire, a little heat in the groin, and before she knew it, her body began moving against him. I shouldn't be doing this, she warned herself as she pulled down the zipper of her sleeping bag. His hands helped her to wrestle clothing out of the way. No caresses. Through it all, she kept her head turned away to avoid his rank tobacco breath.

In the morning, neither mentioned their encounter. Nor did they mention it the next time. Unspoken, what they did in the dark did not officially exist. With heated snow water, she washed her private places as best she could. That was her only acknowledgment, even to herself, of what they did in the night. She noticed that Don now avoided looking her in the eye.

They finished all the rice and macaroni. Only flour and sugar remained.

In the afternoon of the tenth day Heather, wrapped in her sleeping bag, lay on the loveseat, staring up at the spaces between the rafters. It was a day of bitter cold. She tried to think of summer, of green leaves and the smell of grass and the warmth of sunshine on her skin. This effort merely deepened her depression.

Don was in the bedroom, in bed because it was warmer there. She thought about joining him. But the cold pressed down, robbing her of strength to move.

It was a faint humming in the air that first distracted her. Imperceptible at first, it grew louder and louder until she recognized it, unmistakably, as the droning of an airplane.

She turned her head and through the tall windows saw a black shape against the grey sky.

Don rushed from the bedroom, trailing his sleeping bag. He planted his hands on the window glass.

"Cessna," he said. "Single engine."

"Is it coming here?"

"Maybe."

"It is coming here!" As the plane descended, she saw that it was yellow, not black, and that it had skis instead of wheels. She jumped up, ready to run out onto the snow-covered lake, wave her arms and shout: This way! Save me!

Before reaching Osprey Lake, the plane dipped behind the trees and disappeared.

"It's landing on Mud Fish," Don said. "Could be the air ambulance." He lit a cigarette, smoked it to the butt and lit another from it. The engine's drone continued. "The pilot's not sticking around, or he'd kill the engine. He's either letting somebody off or picking somebody up."

A few minutes later the air rumbled as the plane took off. It reappeared above the trees, circled, and headed south. Heather squeezed her eyes shut to stop her tears as she listened to the receding drone.

Don turned to her. "After that excitement, how about something to eat?"

"We've nothing left but sugar and flour."

"Can't you make something out of them?"

"Such as?"

"Bread, maybe?"

"Christ! And you think I'm dumb!"

Heather pulled on the rubber boots, clomped into the kitchen, and lit the Coleman. She broke the skin of ice that had formed over the water in the pail. After pouring water into a saucepan, she stirred in half a cup of flour and a spoonful of sugar.

While waiting for the mixture to come to a boil, she heard Don go outside. It sounded as if he was straightening the woodpile, which was pointless since they couldn't have a fire anyway. By the time he returned, the liquid in the pan had thickened enough to coat a spoon. She sipped a few drops. Awful! But at least it was hot. She filled two mugs and carried them into the main room.

Don stood at the window, looking south at a thick pillar of black smoke rising above the trees.

"Looks like a big fire," she said as she handed him a mug.

"Yeah. Somebody's torched the car." He raised the mug to his lips, grimaced, then drank it in one draught. "Could be Kevin."

"Kevin! You think Kevin was on that plane?" Deep inside her, hope soared like a bird on the wing.

"If it's him, his tracks will lead the cops straight to us. We'll have to clear out."

At last! Heather could hardly breathe for excitement. She didn't care about the cops. She cared about nothing but Kevin, her lover, and leaving this cold wilderness.

"If it's Kevin, how long will it take him to get here?"

"The snow's deep. Maybe half an hour."

Don's cigarette butts were all over the floor. She didn't want Kevin to see a mess like this. She didn't want him to see her like this. She raised her hand to her hair – unwashed for a week – and ran her tongue over her scum-coated teeth – unbrushed for a week. No shower for a week, either.

Heather rushed into the kitchen. There was still some water in the pail. Grabbing a rag, she began to scrub her face and neck. Her skin was stinging when Don shouted, "It's Kevin. He's here."

She dropped the rag and raced into the main room as fast as she could.

Stepping out from the tall pines, Kevin looked like a black cut-out against the white snow. He wore snowshoes, a backpack, and a blue toque pulled low to cover his ears. Always prepared. That was Kevin.

Don rushed to open the door. Barely giving Kevin time to unbuckle his snowshoes, he dragged him inside with a greeting that was half handshake and half bear hug. The quick kiss Kevin gave Heather was partly spoiled by the drip from the end of his nose.

Kevin gazed around the room. "Nothing's changed. It's just the same as when we used to come up here fishing. Remember that?"

"Yeah. I remember."

Heather saw how Don winced. Kevin did not appear to notice.

He slung the backpack from his shoulders. "Here's something to warm us up." He pulled out a tin of coffee and a slightly squashed cardboard box. "Tim Hortons. I figured you guys wouldn't have much food up here."

He opened the box. Within it were a dozen donuts of assorted kinds.

"Oh-my-god!" Heather squealed as she plucked a jelly donut from the box. She licked the smear of raspberry jam, letting the sweetness spread through her mouth. With tiny grunts of pleasure she chewed slowly, rapturously. When the donut was finished, she licked the stickiness from her fingers before retreating to the kitchen with the coffee tin in her hand.

On a shelf she found an old aluminium percolator, the kind with a glass knob on top. As she filled the basket with coffee, she listened to Don and Kevin talking in the main room.

"Why did you risk it?" Don was saying. "You had an alibi."

"Alf couldn't keep his mouth shut. I didn't want you coming back to Toronto with the money." He paused. "You got it, don't you?"

Don's voice was muffled with donut. "Yeah. I got it."

"How much?"

"All of it."

"I said: how much?"

"Two hundred thousand."

Heather nearly dropped the coffee pot.

"Good," Kevin said. "Alf wasn't lying. One hundred thousand for each of us."

"What about Alf?" Don asked. "A third's his."

"Alf's dead."

"That's bad."

"Not as bad as it gets. One of the Paki's friends saw him talking to you. You're the target now. Plus, the surveillance camera got a good shot of you."

"Couldn't have. I had my parka pulled real tight around my face."

"Not tight enough. So the cops are on to you, too."

"What do we do now?" Don asked.

"Disappear."

Heather's hands shook as she lit the Coleman. Who was Alf? She didn't know anybody called Alf. It seemed there was plenty she didn't know.

Don and Kevin lowered their voices. She could not hear what they were saying – just muffled murmurs under the *plop, plop, plop* as percolating coffee sloshed inside the glass knob.

When the coffee was ready, she filled three mugs and placed them on a metal tray.

"Here you are," she said brightly as she carried the tray into the main room and set it on the table. "Fresh and hot."

Neither man smiled.

"Tell her what happened," Don said. He lifted a mug of coffee from the table.

Kevin shrugged. "This guy Alf got a tip that the Paki who owned the Hasti Mart had two hundred thou in fifty-dollar bills, ready for pickup at 1:00 in the morning. Drug money. Me and Don planned to get there first. But the boss called me in to work. I couldn't say no. That's why you had to be the driver."

"Uh-huh," she said. "So now the Paki's friends want the money back?"

"That sums it up." Kevin looked around. "Where is it?"

"In my gym bag." Don said.

"I want to see."

"Don't you trust me?"

"Sure I do. I just need to count it."

"It's all there."

"Don't play games. Get it now."

"All right. All right." Don drained his mug and set it down on the table. "It's in the woodpile." When he went outside, he closed the door behind him.

"He didn't tell me where he hid it," Heather said nervously. "He was afraid I'd go to the cops. He burned my boots so I couldn't leave."

"So that's why you're wearing rubber boots ten sizes too big. You look like a freak."

"It's not like I asked him to burn my boots."

Don came in, slamming the door. He slung the gym bag onto the table.

"Let's see." Kevin unzipped the bag, lifted out the packs of money. He removed the elastic band from one pack and counted the bills. Heather silently counted along with him. Fifty pink banknotes, with the Peace Tower and Mackenzie King on the facing-up side. Kevin pulled out a calculator, punched in numbers.

"It's good." A smile stretched the corners of his mouth.

"What did you expect? I told you it was all there."

Outside the window, shadows deepened under the trees. Soon it would be dark. Kevin returned the money to the gym bag.

"We'll leave tomorrow," Kevin said, "as soon as it's light. A guy in Mud Fish has a jeep. He'll drive you and me to Sudbury. Then we'll catch a bus to Winnipeg and lie low."

"What about her?"

"We aren't safe as long as she's alive."

One moment of incomprehension. Then his meaning struck home. The breath she took was so sharp it staggered her. Heather's mug fell from her hand and shattered on the stone hearth. "No." She grabbed the back of a chair. "No!"

"Christ," Don said. "We don't have to do that."

"We're not taking her with us."

"I could have got rid of her easy on the way up here. I put up with her `cause she's your girlfriend."

"Was." Kevin smiled. "I got a new lady. She'll join us in Winnipeg."

"God! You and your women!"

"Never mind about that. We have to tie this one up. Get some rope."

Don raised both hands shoulder high, palms forward in a gesture that was both protest and surrender. He shook his head as he left the room.

"Let's take care of you," Kevin said, his voice cold as ice.

A punch in the stomach sank her to her knees. Looking up, she saw Don come from the kitchen with a rope over his arm, his eyes avoiding her. He gave the rope to Kevin.

"Give me a hand," Kevin said. He pushed Heather face down on the floor.

"I don't like this," Don said. "We owe her something."

"You've been screwing her, haven't you?"

"No." Don hesitated. "I just think you're overreacting." He stood there, letting Kevin do it all.

Heather felt Kevin's weight on her back, his knees digging into her. He twisted her arms behind her back. The pain was too great to allow room for fear. It was like a knife sawing through her flesh. All she wanted was the pain to stop. Kevin bound her wrists, tied her ankles, and then lashed her wrists and ankles together. Her shoulders strained and her arms nearly pulled from their sockets. Heather was panting for breath.

Kevin stood up, laughing. "Overreacting? Who, me? You're the one that killed the Paki. Bashed in his skull."

"Self-defence."

"Right. The Paki was how tall? Five-foot-four? And about fifty years old."

"He was just a Paki. Heather's one of us."

"Don't be stupid. We gotta do it."

Don's voice was very quiet. "How?"

"A fire. We torch the cottage."

"No. Not that way."

"Okay. We leave her here, tied up." He laughed. "Freeze-dried, she won't talk."

"She'll be easy to identify," Don said.

"All right. How do we get rid of a body? We can't bury her; the earth's like concrete."

"There's an outhouse. We could throw her into the pit."

Along with the ancestors' bones, she thought. Well, what did it matter?

"Too slow," Kevin said. "Maybe we could cut a hole in the ice, weigh her down and shove her under. By the time she came up, there wouldn't be enough left to identify."

They were talking about her as if she didn't exist. Death by fire. Death by cold. Her body thrown into the outhouse pit or abandoned under a foot of ice. Heather pulled air into her lungs. She screamed. No words. Just a scream.

"That does it," Kevin said. "Find something to gag her while I pour more coffee."

As night fell, Heather gradually became aware that she was no longer cold. The shuddering in her limbs had stopped. The ropes that bound her wrists and ankles ceased to hurt.

Moonlight flooded through the windows. Even at the back of the room, near the fireplace, shapes were distinguishable from shadows. From where she lay, her right cheek on the floorboards, Heather could see the gym bag on the floor by the back door.

In the bedroom, Kevin and Don had been quarrelling. Heather had heard a few shouted words, enough to know that Don was "really pissed off" and that Kevin "hadn't realized Don was such an asshole".

But the argument had stopped. Probably both had fallen asleep. Soon she would be sleeping too, but with a difference. In the morning they would wake up, and she would not. Already languor spread through her veins.

Heather had never thought much about death, her own death. Sometimes she thought about her life, with Kevin as its centre. All that was best and worst was wrapped up in him. Yet the more she loved him, the more he took advantage. Why had she expected that to change? And now it had come to this. In the cold cottage, without a sleeping bag, she would die before morning. But she didn't care much. Death might not be so bad. She sure had made a total mess of life. Her blind obedience filled her with disgust and shame that she had kept on doing for Kevin things that she did not want to do.

From the bedroom came the creak of the mattress. She knew that sound – how it squeaked when you sat up, squeaked again when you rose from bed. Was that Kevin or Don getting up? She could not see the bedroom door from where she lay, trussed like a chicken.

The floor creaked. She stiffened, her lethargy gone. Now into her field of vision moved the dark shape of a man. He wore a backpack and a toque, and he carried his boots in one hand.

At the back door he bent over the gym bag and picked it up.

Heather held her breath, willing him to open the door. Dear God, let him go! Let him take the money! If it was just her and Don, she had a chance.

Kevin's hand was on the doorknob when the gun went off. It knocked him sideways and hurled him to the floor.

So the gun was real.

Now she could see Don, the weapon in his hand, come from the bedroom, walk up to Kevin, and stand over him.

"You greedy bastard," Don said.

She thought he was about to fire again, but the gun wavered. Kevin had not moved. Don turned his head. Heather felt his eyes on her.

"Kevin didn't give a damn about either of us. He wanted everything for himself. That's why he came up here. To take it all."

Heather's response was a muffled grunt.

"Oh!" Don sounded dazed. "The gag."

Turning his back as he set the gun on the mantel, Don did not see Kevin rise on one elbow. Heather did. She saw him slip one hand inside his jacket. She tried to scream.

The report was hardly more than a popgun's bang. Don wheeled, clutched his belly, and fell to his knees.

Kevin's second shot went wild. Window glass shattered. The gun fell from his hand. This time he remained still.

Don sat down heavily, his arms wrapped around his abdomen. His voice, when it came, was thick with pain. "I should have finished the job, but I couldn't. Not close up, seeing his face. We were friends a long time."

He tried to haul himself to his feet by holding onto a chair, but his strength failed. Crawling to Heather, he untied the rope that pulled back the corners of her mouth and then pulled out the wad of rags that Kevin had stuffed inside. She gulped, tried to speak, but her mouth was too dry. She swallowed again, moving her tongue till saliva flowed.

"Untie me. I'll get help."

She heard his harsh breathing at her back as his fingers fumbled with the rope. "Damn it. The knots are too tight."

"Use a knife."

"Yeah. I'll do that. There's a penknife on my key chain. Just a minute."

It took a very long minute for his knife to scrape through the ropes.

By the time she was free, the sky outside the windows was no longer dark. Dawn had arrived, and with it more snow – hard, icy grains that the wind swept against the glass.

By the back door lay Kevin's body. Blood splattered his face, his clothes, and the gym bag. It coated the floor like fresh red paint. Heather stumbled to him and knelt by his side. In death he was as handsome as ever. The bullet had entered one side of his neck and emerged on the other, leaving his face unmarred. She touched his hand. It was still warm, yet the feel of his once-loved skin brought no reaction. If love was a sickness, she was cured.

She turned toward Don. "I can walk to that village. I'll wear Kevin's snowshoes. You told me the people have snowmobiles."

"Don't go."

"You need help."

"Stay with me." He was sitting on the floor. His hands, covered with blood, clutched his stomach as if he were trying to hold it in. "Light me a smoke."

His cigarettes lay on the table beside his lighter. When she had lit one, she handed it to him. He sucked as a baby sucks milk. The colour had drained from his narrow face, but his dark eyes burned as fiercely as before.

"Where's the nearest hospital?" she asked.

"Huntsville. Two hours by snowmobile. I'd never make it."

When she saw how the cigarette wobbled in his fingers, she took it from him and stubbed it on the floor.

"My brother Charlie died here."

"The boy in the photograph?"

"Yeah. He was twelve. He'd bugged Kevin and me to bring him up here when we went fishing. We didn't want him, but Dad said we had to take him along. We paddled over to the village and bought a couple of forty-ouncers from Rosemary Bear Paw. Charlie'd never had a drink before. We thought he went outside to throw up. Drowned in six inches of water right by the shore."

"You don't need to tell me."

Don's chest rose and fell. His voice rasped. "It wasn't my fault. What kind of parents would throw out a seventeen-year-old kid because of an accident? When I phoned my grandfather, he hung up on me. It's their fault I ended up on the street." His eyebrows lifted up. The dark eyes that once looked right through her were clouded now. "Bear Paw ... take you to the bus ... blue house." His eyes closed. "Will you do me a favour?"

"Sure."

"Burn the cottage. Do that for me. When my dad and my uncle finish suing each other, the winner gets a pile of ashes. Serve the bastards right."

Don's head fell back and his body slid sideways. Heather put her arm around the back of his neck to support him. A single breath shuddered from his chest. She counted the seconds, waiting for the next breath. It didn't come.

Snow blowing in through the broken window sifted like salt across the floor. Heather unscrewed the top of the kerosene can she had found in the junk room. Starting at the back door, she poured kerosene onto the floor, pacing a circle around the room, both bodies within its circumference.

She had Kevin's boots on her feet. Although large, they weren't as huge as the size-thirteen rubber boots. She would have taken his toque as well, if it had not been soaked with blood.

Completion of the circle returned her to the back door, where the gym bag lay. Maybe she should try to sponge off the blood, but she did not want to take the time. When did the bus go through Huntsville? Or was there a closer stop, a depot in some country store along the way? Rosemary Bear Paw would know. Heather glanced at her wristwatch. Eight o'clock. Time to get moving.

With a flick of Don's lighter, she lit a candle end. It was a stubby candle that would stand upright without a holder. She set it down carefully on the kerosene trail. In five minutes, ten at most, the flame would burn down to the kerosene.

Heather picked up the gym bag and opened the door. She whacked Kevin's snowshoes against the wall to shake off the snow before buckling them on.

The wind slammed into her face. It howled across the lake, lashing her cheeks with icy grains that stung like needles. The osprey nest at the top of the dead pine rocked in the gale.

Heather plodded through the snow, her bare head bent to the wind. When she stopped to look back, the cottage's tall windows were aglow.

Was the cottage insured? Or would Don's father and uncle really be left with only a pile of ashes to fight over? That was none of her concern. Heather had her own money to think about. Two hundred thousand dollars would take care of her for a long time. She didn't need much – just a small apartment with a bathroom. Tub and shower. Fluffy towels. A nice kitchen with lots of cupboards to store the food she would buy. Kraft dinners. Chocolate chip cookies. The thought cheered her as she trudged on.

Heather wasn't sure where she wanted the bus to carry her. The further from Toronto, the better. Kevin had mentioned Sudbury. A real city. Big enough to get lost in. She wouldn't want to live in some little town where everybody knew everybody else's business.

Unaccustomed to snowshoes, Heather found it hard going to place one foot in front of the other. When she was halfway to the end of the lake, a stitch in her side forced her to stop. Glancing back at the cottage, she saw flames shooting from the windows, and she fought the image of Kevin and Don sprawled on the floor. Kevin had it coming. Don was a loser, but he didn't deserve to die. She and Don might have got along if they had stuck together. Who knew? It couldn't happen, anyway.

She trudged on. The exertion brought some warmth to her body. Managing the snowshoes also grew easier. Nearing the village, she saw that each shanty had a snowmobile parked near its door. Every house but one looked as though no paintbrush had ever touched it. That one exceptional house was blue.

Heather stumbled onto the shore. Setting down the gym bag, she reached into her pocket for a tissue to wipe her dripping nose.

There was no sign of life in any of the houses. Outside the blue house, a scruffy dog lifted its leg against a yellow and black snowmobile. When the dog had finished, it trotted to the house, acknowledging her with a glance over its shoulder. At the door it gave a sharp bark. The door opened to admit the dog, then closed.

Heather picked up the gym bag and tramped to the house. At her knock, the door opened again with a blast of warm air that smelled of tobacco and smoked fish. Before her stood an enormous woman wearing a lumberjack shirt. She had a neck like a bull, and her shoulders sloped. Her face was coppery brown with wide cheekbones. Beady eyes imbedded in fat pouches regarded Heather with more suspicion than surprise. At her feet, the dog growled.

"Where'd you come from?" The woman had a tiny Cupid's bow mouth that scarcely opened when she spoke.

"Across the lake. I … uh … need a ride to the bus."

The woman eyed Heather from head to foot. She saw it all: the bomber jacket, the tight jeans, the men's boots, and the blood-splattered gym bag.

"I'll take you over for fifty bucks."

"Fine."

The woman opened the door wider. "Come inside before all the heat gets out."

Heather kicked off the snowshoes and stepped into a small room that was almost filled by the woman's bulk. In one corner stood a cast iron stove. A yellow glow outlined the rectangle of the door in its side. On top of the stove a copper kettle steamed. A bed covered by a red blanket pressed against one wall. Near the opposite wall stood a wooden table and three chairs that did not match.

"Are you Rosemary Bear Paw?"

"You know my name? You come from Carsons' place, I think." Her dark eyes studied Heather's face. "I knew somebody was staying there. It don't take much to tell me that. I don't ask questions." Her eyes dropped to the blood-splashed gym bag. "Been plenty trouble there already."

She lowered her bulk onto the bed and pulled on her boots, huffing as she leaned forward to lace them. "That hillside, in the old days we buried our people there. Sacred land. My father told Mr. Carson not to dig there, but he don't listen." With a grunt, she stood up and pulled her parka from a hook. "That Carson boy and his friend used to come up here to get drunk. They said they come to fish, but I don't see nobody put their line in the water. Then the little kid drowned. That killed the old man."

She wrestled her arms into the parka's sleeves. "For eight years, I see no family there. Some day that place burn down." She finished with a pucker of her lips and a popping sound, like a kiss.

The woman held out her hand, which was dimpled and remarkably small, considering the size of her body. "Fifty dollars. Then I take you."

Heather handed over two twenties and a ten. The money went straight into a coffee tin on the table. Rosemary Bear Paw pulled on a pair of leather gauntlets decorated with bright beadwork: red, green, and white.

"We go before anybody wake up."

Heather looked around but saw no sign of another person in the house.

"I mean neighbours. They still sleeping it off. They don't need to know you been here."

Heather picked up the gym bag.

The dog followed them to the door and looked up expectantly. "Not this time," the woman said. "Go lie down." The dog trotted over to the stove and flopped onto the floor.

As soon as she stepped outside, Rosemary Bear Paw saw the tower of flames that rose as high as the treetops above the Carson cottage. She stopped, watched for half a minute.

"Huh! I tell you, the shadows of the ancestors never leave this land."

They can keep it, Heather thought. This was one place she never wanted to see again.

The snowmobile looked like a monster insect. No, not exactly an insect. More like that contraption the Space Centre sent up to Mars. It was a new machine, and probably worth more than all the houses of the village put together.

"You like it, eh? Ski-Doo Skandic SUV. Top of the line."

The passenger seat had a tiny backrest and handgrips at the sides. Behind the seat was an open luggage basket.

"Put your bag in there."

Heather shook her head. No way she was going to put two hundred thousand dollars into an open bin where it might bounce out any time the snowmobile hit a bump. If that happened, she wouldn't know the bag was gone until she reached her destination.

"I'll hold it on my lap."

"There's no room."

This was obvious. Behind the driver, there was room only for Heather on the saddle seat. But to leave the gym bag in an open rack! Forget it!

"Let's go," the woman grunted. "We don't have all day."

Heather made no move to put the gym bag into the basket.

"All right. All right. If it makes you feel better, there's storage under the seat."

Why hadn't she said that to start with? Under the seat, weighed down by the driver's three hundred pounds, plus Heather's less significant one hundred and ten, the money would be safe.

"Give me your bag. I'll put it in for you."

"No! No! I can do it myself."

"What you got in there? Drugs?"

"Just some clothes."

"Huh! They must be pretty nice clothes."

Rosemary Bear Paw's tiny mouth pursed as she watched Heather tuck the gym bag into the storage area. After putting back the seat, she said only, "Let's go."

For a moment, as she climbed aboard, Heather thought of asking if she could go back and use the bathroom. But the thought of another hole in a board over a stinking pit was too gross.

"Is it far to the bus station?" she asked, picturing a modern facility, with ceramic tiles, flush toilets, clean sinks, and taps that flowed with hot and cold running water.

"Not far." Rosemary Bear Paw started the engine.

The hills that rose up on either side seemed to funnel the Ski-Doo from lake to lake. The wind screamed in Heather's ears. One lake led into another, and then another. No sign of a highway, a road or a town. Heather saw nothing but rocks, trees, and the occasional boarded-up summer cottage.

If she had known it would take this long, she definitely would have asked to use the washroom. Her bladder pressed sorely. The vibration of the machine made it worse. Heather panicked. What if she wet herself? She would rather die than go into a bus depot with pee leaked all over her pants.

By the time she let go of the right hand grip to thump Rosemary Bear Paw on the back, it was nearly too late.

The snowmobile stopped, its motor still turning over. The woman shouted over her shoulder, "What's your problem?"

"I need to pee."

"Help yourself." Her tiny mouth spat out the words.

Heather dismounted and waded off through the snow. When she was a few yards behind the snowmobile, she unzipped her jeans. Rosemary Bear Paw swivelled on her seat to watch. Did she expect Heather to pee while being stared at? She felt like screaming: *Turn your goddamn back!* Not until Heather's panties and jeans were around her ankles did the woman turn around.

Such a relief to release the flow, to feel the pressure ease! As her bladder emptied, Heather relaxed as much as anyone could relax while squatting bare-bottomed in the snow.

The revving of the motor took her by surprise. She was still peeing when the engine roared and the Ski-Doo sped away.

"Hey! Wait a minute!" she shouted, as if the snowmobile's departure were mere carelessness – a failure to notice that the passenger was not on board.

It took Heather ten seconds to realize that the snowmobile was not going to stop, another ten to claw her clothing into place. She chased after the Ski-Doo, stumbling through the snow and hollering, "Don't leave me here!" The diminishing roar of its motor hummed in her ears long after it had disappeared behind a hill.

After disbelief, shock set in. The gym bag was gone. The money was gone. And she was alone in the middle of a frozen lake. The Ski-Doo's track, a long scar in the white snow, was the only sign that anyone other than Heather had been here. Everything else seemed like a bad dream. Only the track was real. She had to follow that track, and quickly, before drifting snow erased it.

Which way should she go? Forward or back?

Osprey Lake was too far back for her to walk. And even if she reached it, why should she expect help from anyone who lived there? She would go forward, she decided.

There would be a town beyond the next hill. She would come upon it soon.

Snow swirled in every direction. Drifts soon covered the snowmobile's track. In front of her, sky and snow formed a single white wall.

Heather walked and walked until she lost all sense of time and place. There was a buzzing in her head. Images swam vaguely in her mind. For a while, someone seemed to walk beside her, a presence felt rather than seen. When she turned her head to see, nothing was there but swirling snow.

As the sky darkened, a heavy drowsiness came upon her. She let her knees give way and her body sink into the softness of the snow. Rest and sleep, she thought. Rest and sleep. Memories passed through her mind like strands of mist, like fragments of a dream. It was summer, and Kevin lay beside her on the plaid blanket, down by a river, just past a little town that was out of sight behind a hill. She made an effort to touch his face. But she was too tired.

There were voices in the wind. They came from above her and from every side, chanting in a language she did not know. She heard drums too, but that might have been her blood beating in her ears, fainter now and far away.

Devotion

"You saw Martin?" Elinor said.

Forrest Parker nodded. "I saw him with my own eyes."

"At Toronto Airport?"

"Picking up his suitcase from the carousel."

"How can you be sure it was Martin, after fifteen years?"

"How could I not recognize my own brother?"

"It's impossible. Martin is dead."

"If you doubt my word …"

"It's not your word I doubt. Your eyesight, perhaps, but not your word."

Forrest wore thick glasses, the lenses so thick that his blue eyes looked like objects seen through the wrong end of a telescope. The only time he took off his glasses was when he went to bed.

"This not a joke," he said. "I came straight from the airport to tell you."

Her hand shook as she set down her cup and saucer. "Did he recognize you … this man you think was Martin?"

"No. I'm sure he didn't see me. He was watching for his luggage. Just as I noticed him, his suitcase came around the carousel; he grabbed it and rushed off."

"Did you follow him, or notice where he went?"

"I was too astonished to do anything. And then he was gone."

"You're sure it was Martin?"

"Absolutely. I had a perfect view. I was standing at the next carousel. My flight from Chicago arrived about fifteen minutes after his flight from Honduras."

"Honduras! What on earth would Martin be doing there?"

"Avoiding extradition, is my guess."

"Then they were right – all the people who said his disappearance was a hoax."

"You have to admit that he had ample reason to disappear."

"I know," she said, and then, "I was certain that if he was alive, he would manage somehow to get word to me. For years I jumped every time the telephone rang."

"I realize that. You waited until there wasn't a grain of hope left."

She looked up sharply. "And now he has come back. I wonder why."

"I expect you and I will find out before long. Whatever the reason for his return, the two people he's most likely to contact are his brother and his wife."

"I'm no longer his wife. Legally, I'm his widow."

"True. But I'm still his brother." Forrest looked at his watch. "It's four o'clock. Time I dropped by the office to see what appointments I have for tomorrow. How about I pick you up at seven? We'll go out for dinner. I'll spend the night here."

"That's not necessary."

"For your protection."

She shook her head. "I'm in no danger."

"What will you do if Martin shows up on your doorstep?"

"I'll deal with that when and if it happens. I can't expect you to spend every night with me on the chance he might come here."

"I have no objection. Far from it."

"No. Not tonight. You look as if you need to rest, after three days of listening to lectures about teeth."

"Isn't this something that you and I should face together?" He shrugged when she did not answer. "Tomorrow, then. Seven o'clock."

Elinor did not rise from her chair when he left.

For a long time she remained sitting while her mind replayed the events of the day that Martin disappeared. It had been fifteen years ago, yet everything remained as sharp in her memory as if it had happened last week.

It had been the fourth day of their holiday in Costa Rica. For the first three days, Martin had been unable to relax. Then overnight his mood changed and he had become very calm. Whatever stress he had been under seemed to have melted away. In the afternoon, Elinor told him she was going to walk along the beach to Puerto Viejo to buy sunscreen at the *farmacia*. He was lying in a hammock reading a magazine. "I don't feel like going for a walk," he had told her. "Maybe a swim after I've finished reading this article."

Two hours later, she returned to the hotel to find him missing. He was not on the beach, in the hotel gardens, or in the bar. It was only when a fellow guest recalled having seen him on the beach wearing his swimming trunks, that she felt anxious enough to report Martin's absence to the hotel desk. The search began at once and continued until darkness fell.

She did not join the search, but sat on the trunk of a fallen palm tree, numb with fear. The hotel owner himself brought her a drink of water.

"Do you think they'll find my husband?" she asked.

The hotel owner sat down beside her. "I'll be open with you, Mrs. Parker. A swimmer caught in an undertow is seldom seen again."

The next day Forrest arrived from Canada. He dealt with all the required formalities and then took her home.

Forrest was Martin's older brother. Though his elder by only two years, he had always looked out for Martin, having assumed the protector role at the age of nine, after their father's death. When Martin married, Forrest extended his protection to Elinor. He had never married, leading her to assume that he was gay. But when Martin died – if he did die – Forrest transferred all his attention to her. After a decent interval, she discovered that he was not gay.

Forrest was a dentist, a serious man who paid attention to details. She enjoyed his company. The fact that he wanted to marry her was flattering, but she liked her life the way it was.

"You're heartless," he said when she turned him down for the second time.

Elinor supposed there might be some truth to this. She knew that she was not a woman of strong passions. Forrest had said she reminded him of porcelain. Elinor, to whom the image suggested a Royal Doulton figurine, appreciated the compliment. Her skin was smooth and luminous, her movements graceful. If it were not for the existence of a twenty-year-old son and an eighteen-year-old daughter, no one would take her for a day over thirty-five.

Elinor loved her orderly life and her beautiful home in Oakville. It was the home she had lived in since 1985, when Martin had bought it for cash. In those days, she had little idea what her husband did for a living, except that he invested people's money for them and was apparently very good at it.

Only later, after his disappearance, did the facts come out. Martin's investment business was a Ponzi scheme. He had defrauded his investors – many of them his friends – of seven million dollars. Several of his victims phoned Elinor to tell her that they would gladly murder him if he were not, as they thought, already dead.

Martin had taken out life insurance. Two million dollars, with double indemnity in case of accidental death. After his disappearance, she had filed her claim. But Beneficent Life, receiving no evidence that Martin had died, accidentally or otherwise, would not pay. Unable to provide any proof of death, Elinor would be forced to wait seven years for Martin to be certified as legally dead.

In cases of plane crashes and natural disasters where bodies were unrecoverable, her lawyer told her, a judge had the discretionary power to speed up the process of issuing a death certificate. Her lawyer made the application. The judge turned it down.

The insurance company fought her all the way. When the seven years had passed, Beneficent Life argued that Martin had voided the policy by committing suicide.

Throughout her legal battles, true-blue Forrest stood by her side.

"Keep your life as normal as possible," had been his advice, "for the children's sake as well as your own."

Since this advice accorded with her own wishes, she kept her pleasant part-time job in a local art gallery. Finally, after ten years of legal wrangling, she received the four-million-dollar insurance benefit.

Like an earthquake, Martin's reappearance would shatter everything.

At the art gallery the next morning, arranging pictures for an exhibition, Elinor tried to shut out all thoughts of Martin. By three o'clock, when her workday ended, she had come close to persuading herself that Forrest, with his challenged eyesight, must be wrong.

On her way home she stopped at Heads Up Salon for her weekly appointment. Relaxing while the stylist created fresh highlights in her blond hair, she looked forward to dinner with Forrest. Maybe he would be less certain about having seen Martin. Then they could relax and get back to normal again.

She had driven her BMW into the garage and turned off the ignition when she saw Martin standing beside the door that gave entry to the house. His finger was on the button to close the garage door. Before she had time to react, the door rumbled down.

She sat rigid, sick with apprehension as Martin approached the driver-side window and peered at her through the glass. His face was pale and deeply lined, his eyes sunk in shadow. His skin sagged. Stubble the colour of cigarette ash covered his cheeks and chin. He looked older than his fifty years. Older than Forrest.

For an instant, she felt that her heart had stopped.

"Elinor, I didn't mean to give you a shock ..."

He had to shout, the window being closed.

She opened the window by a hand's breadth. "You didn't." She tried to keep her voice steady. "Forrest told me that he saw you yesterday at Pearson Airport. He said your flight came from Honduras."

It was Martin who looked shocked. The news seemed to knock him off balance. He reached out one hand, placing it on the window's lower ledge. Elinor noticed that his fingernails were untrimmed.

"Since we have to talk," she said, "we might as well go in the house. Forrest is coming over at seven. He was planning to take me out to dinner." Was, she thought. Everything was different now.

Elinor felt nervous as she opened the car door. Martin followed closely as they went into the house. Only when they entered the kitchen did she begin to relax. This was familiar ground.

"The house is in nice shape," he said. "I've had a look around."

"How did you get in?"

"I still have a key." He reached into his back pants' pocket, pulled out a brass key. As he gave it to her, she saw how his hand shook. "You can have it back."

She set the key on the table. "I'm amazed you kept it all these years. There's no chance you can ever live in this house again."

"I never thought I could." He held out one hand, palm up, as if in supplication. "May we discuss this over a drink? You make the best martini."

She hesitated. A drink might keep their discussion civilized until Forrest arrived. Whatever was to be done, Forrest would have to be part of it.

"Very well."

She took the vodka from the refrigerator, poured four ounces into a measuring cup, added vermouth, and stirred.

"No olive, correct?"

"Correct."

She poured their drinks into martini glasses and set them on the kitchen table.

They sat down facing each other.

"Why did you come back?"

"For you. For fifteen years, not a day has passed without my thinking of you."

Elinor waited. Had there been no women in Honduras to distract him? She knew that she could have managed celibacy if she had tried. But not Martin, whose sexual needs were much stronger than hers.

"I thought of you standing on the beach," he said, "your long hair blowing. How different our lives should have been! I ought to have been with you to raise our children. Living in Honduras, I missed all that."

She felt like telling him that he would have been in prison for those fifteen years, and how much parenting could he have contributed from a cell?

All she said was, "Yes, you missed all that. Mike and Nelly are no longer children. They're both away at university."

"Where?"

"I'm not going to tell you. I don't want you anywhere near either of them."

"What do they know about me?"

"About your crime? Nothing, though sooner or later someone is sure to tell them what you did. All they know is that you loved them."

"That is the truth, or part of it."

"Then leave them alone. Let them go on thinking that you died. When they were little, they used to look at pictures in our photo albums of all of us together. A beautiful family. Mike would tell Nelly what he remembered about you. She can't remember you at all."

"I don't suppose I'd recognize either of them if I saw them walking in the street. But it's really you I came for. As long as I have you, I'm ready to let them live their own lives."

She sat there with her hands cupped around her glass. This was bizarre, she thought. He was living in a fantasy if he thought that she would have him back.

"There are two ways we can handle this," he said. "The best way is simple. You go to Honduras on vacation. You meet me. I court you. We marry."

She drained her glass. He's crazy, she thought.

"Or we could stay in Canada. That would carry more risk. Of course I have a new identity." He laughed. "My name is Richard Mann. I was born in Brandon, Manitoba."

He pulled a navy-blue passport from his pocket and opened it to the first page.

"See. That's my picture."

She nodded. It was his picture.

"We can't live anyplace in the Toronto area," he continued, "where somebody might recognize me. But Mr. and Mrs. Richard Mann would have all the rest of the country to choose from."

"Yes. I suppose so." She had to stall, she thought, until Forrest arrived. Martin's brother could handle him if anyone could. The clock read 6:00 p.m. One more hour.

"Did you say that Forrest would be here at seven?"

Oh, my God, she thought. Can Martin read my mind?

"I don't want to see him." Martin finished his drink and set down the glass.

"You might as well, since he already knows that you've come back."

"You told me. But Forrest has no part in my plans." Martin shook his head, as if to clear his mind. "This throws a spanner in the works."

She did not understand what he meant.

"When he gets here," she said, "the three of us can discuss the situation. Like a family."

Martin's hands trembled like an old man's. There was all the difference in the world between the man she had married and this wreck sitting at her kitchen table. Only his eyes were the same – as long as she looked directly at his eyes and not at the dark shadows under them – a unique shade somewhere between grey and green. She had loved the colour of his eyes.

He used to be so well-groomed, she thought. Fingernails trimmed. Clean-shaven. If he isn't broke, why doesn't he take better care of himself? Maybe he slept rough last night, afraid to go to a hotel for fear of being recognized. That could explain it.

"Good old Forrest," Martin said. "Always there to lend a helping hand."

"While we wait, you might tell me how you managed to disappear? I'd like to know what really happened."

"Nothing too complicated. While you were walking into Puerto Viejo, I put on my swim trunks and lounged around on the beach for long enough that a dozen people could swear they saw me. Then I sneaked into the bushes to change into some regular clothes I had hidden there earlier with my passport and my money."

Your clients' money, she thought.

"After changing, I walked to Cahuita. There was little traffic. Whenever a car or a bicycle came along, I ducked into the bushes. From Cahuita, I caught the bus to Puerto Limon. American dollars can get you anything in Puerto Limon. Women. Drugs. Men with fast boats. I hired a man who took me north. We dodged the Nicaraguan Coast Guard. At night he landed me at a small Honduran port."

Elinor's voice shook. "All that time, people were searching for you. When the tide came in, I thought of your body washing up on the beach. But you were alive, and you never let me know."

"Elinor, there was no way I could have let you know. I had to think about the insurance. If it became known that I sent a message during the seven years after my disappearance, the death certificate would not be issued and you would have received no benefits. Besides that, if you concealed knowledge that I was alive, you could be charged with collusion. Sorry. I had to do it that way in order to provide for my family."

"If that's your way of providing for your family, you have a badly skewed sense of responsibility."

"It worked, didn't it? As long as Martin Parker remains dead, the money is yours."

Yes, she thought, as long as he remains dead. "Let's have another martini while we decide what to do." She managed a smile. "I could certainly use one."

"So could I," he said.

She rose from her chair and picked up both empty glasses. A wooden knife stand stood on the counter, inches from the bottle of vodka and the bottle of vermouth. In the stand was a long, sharp knife.

Martin's back was to the counter. His shoulders were bent, his head lowered.

She pulled the knife from the rack and plunged it into his back with all her force, pulled it free and stabbed again.

His bright blood spurted over her clothes and over the counter. It splashed the liquor bottles and the two martini glasses.

For a long time she clung to the knife. There was silence, apart from the clock's ticking.

Martin's body was still slumped over the table. She noticed that his neck was thin and his hair very grey. Slowly she set down the knife a few inches from his head. Because she could not think what else to do, she continued to stand there, leaning back against the counter.

The doorbell rang. That would be Forrest. He always rang and waited for her to let him in. It was part of his courtesy, an acknowledgement that this was her domain. But he had a key. After he had rung a second time, he let himself in.

Forrest took one step into the kitchen and then stood perfectly still. He opened his mouth, and his voice croaked out.

"What happened?"

"An intruder. It was self-defence." It surprised her that she could talk, although she heard the quaver in her voice. She was almost without feeling, too numb for pain or fear. "He told me his name was Richard Mann. He showed me his passport."

"Did you touch it?"

"No. He opened it, showed me the first page, then put it back in his pocket."

"I'll take one of your shower curtains to wrap him," Forrest said. "We'll put him in the trunk of your car. After we've cleaned everything up, we'll go for a drive. There's a swamp in Flamborough, close to a road that's seldom used."

Elinor nodded, aware that her body had started to tremble now that there was no need to be strong. She could let Forrest take over. Soon life would be normal again.

Her Ideal Man, Sublime

I had a lover named Jerome, but he developed a plantar wart on his foot. Every time I thought about that wart, my insides twisted. I never let on how it bothered me. The wart was not Jerome's fault, although it was a fault in him. I found some other excuse for breaking up.

I tell Dr. Freitag about this. They take me to see her every week. Tuesdays at ten o'clock. She is a small, dark woman with greying hair pulled tight in a bun and a faint moustache above her upper lip. She is writing a book about people like me, people whose powers cannot be explained by physical science. I have volunteered my expertise to help her with the final draft of her manuscript.

Dr. Freitag sits behind her desk and I sit in a chair in front. We talk about books and movies, and she asks me about the kind of thing I like. I tell her that my favourite film is Casablanca.

She asks, "What do you like most about it?"

"The ending is perfect," I explain. "Rick will never see Ilsa's beauty fade. She will never know if he develops a wart on his foot. They will always have Paris."

Dr. Freitag blinks her eyes but she doesn't comment.

After Jerome, I avoided physical intimacy in my relationships. In fact, I avoided relationships altogether. They were right, those old Gnostics who thought that the spirit is imprisoned in the flesh. The more I saw of people's messy lives, the more disgusted I became. If I had been the Creator of the whole human race, I would have done a better job.

At work, I kept to myself. When my co-workers at Erskine Press saw me in the lunchroom with my sandwich and apple and my book open on my lap, they thought I was reading. But in that stuffy lunchroom I overheard such confidences as you could not imagine. For example, the elegant Delia Jones' ex-husband made wife-swapping arrangements through the Internet and told Delia she had to go along because their marriage was finished if she refused. I wish I could have been a fly on the wall during that conversation!

After twenty years at Erskine, I knew everything about my co-workers, but they knew nothing about me. To them, I was just a proofreader. As if that weren't the most important job at any publishing house! The last line of defence against error. I was the one who ensured that Erskine books were perfect when they reached the reader's hands. Only a person of some genius can do that.

I know what they thought of me. "Poor old Edna," I heard them say. They had a nickname for me: Brunhilde. This was inspired, I suppose, by my imposing appearance. I am tall and big-boned, with broad shoulders and fair hair. Goddess-like. Ignoring the spirit of mockery in which it was applied, I took the nickname as a compliment.

My co-workers' experiences interested me. It was fascinating to watch the unravelling of their tangled affairs. I have always been a student of other people's lives. That was why I bought the binoculars.

Before I was sent to Penetanguishene, I lived in Toronto in an apartment building that was constructed like three sides of a square, the open end facing St. Clair Avenue. My apartment was in the east wing, on the 7th floor. Whenever the occupants left their drapes open, I had a clear view from my living room into four west-wing apartments.

The lenses of my binoculars must have reflected light, because one evening at sunset a man waved to me from the living-room window of the apartment directly across from mine. Then he slowly took off his shirt, making a big show of it. Next he let his pants drop. When he was totally nude, he grabbed his penis and waggled it at me. I was never so shocked in my life. Some very weird people lived in that building

I put away the binoculars. For months they remained unused in the drawer of my bedside table. I did not miss them. Anthony had entered my life.

Very few people possess the power to bring an idea into being. It so happens that I am one of them. This is a power that I have always enjoyed. As a child five years old, I had a best friend who was invisible to everyone but me. Her name was Susan.

Dr. Freitag wants to know all about Susan. I am happy to oblige. I tell her that Susan had physical reality: hair and skin, hands and feet, scabs on her knees like all little girls. She talked and laughed and sang and sometimes cried. Then one day she left. Poof! She was gone.

Dr. Freitag is not surprised. "That happens," she says, and takes a few notes. Nothing surprises Dr. Freitag. I don't know how much I'm going to tell her about Anthony. She is a spider trying to draw me into her web to suck my blood. But I am wilier than she thinks.

Anthony sprang from my brain like Pallas Athene from the mind of Zeus, fully grown and armed. He had dark, wavy hair and an aquiline nose from his Italian mother, and intense blue eyes from his Austrian father. He wore a well-cut suit and carried not a sword, but a black briefcase.

Our relationship was transcendental, a love that lay beyond and above the limits of material experience. A union not of the body but of the mind. That is to say, it was between our perfect selves. Anthony explained that he had created me just as I had created him. We were each the creature of the other's brain. That's how I knew we were gods. Who but a god could create a human being out of nothing?

"You are mine and I am yours," he told me one night as I lay in his arms. "There will never be another woman in my life."

Everything was perfect. The love we shared excelled any physical love whose soul is sense. I believed that we were inseparable. But one day, inexplicably, he was gone. For weeks I wandered about my apartment, disconsolate, talking out loud, listening in vain for an answering voice. It's happened again, I thought, just like Susan, my childhood friend. It seemed that, though I had the power to bring people into being, I could not keep them from slipping away again.

At our next session I explain this to Dr. Freitag. She nods her head slowly. "I see," she says, "but it's not such a problem as you think. You invented Anthony because you needed him. When your need ceased, he ceased to exist." She is so wrong! Anthony has not ceased to exist.

About two months after Anthony's disappearance, his picture appeared in the *Toronto Star*. I knew at once that this was Anthony, even though the caption identified him as Robert Jamieson, the spokesman for some charity. The picture had been taken at a Toronto fund-raising event. He wore a tuxedo and, so far as I could tell, was not carrying his briefcase. In the photograph a woman stood at his side. She was blond and petite, with long hair and sharp features. I did not notice her name because it did not matter.

Six months later, on my way home from work, I saw Anthony again. He was waiting on the subway platform at the College station, and this time he was carrying his black briefcase.

I entered the car behind him, instantly resolving to get off when he did and follow him wherever he went. But, to my delight, he got off at St. Clair, the same stop as mine. I kept a few paces behind him. When he crossed at my crossing, I began to suspect that we lived in the same apartment building. If so, he must be a new tenant. Today was the 4th of October. He must have moved in on the first of the month.

I slipped into the building right after him and stood beside him in the crowded elevator. My heart pounded so loudly that I thought everyone in the elevator might be able to hear. But Anthony's glance passed over me as if I were invisible. My lover, my soulmate, pretended not to know me.

I wanted to ask why he had withdrawn so abruptly from my life and what he had been doing for the past eight months. Yet I resisted. Instead of demanding an answer, I must try to learn more about what was happening in his life.

When he stepped out of the elevator at the 6th floor, I followed at a discreet distance. At a door near the end of the hall, he stopped and took out his key. After he had gone inside, I walked past the door he had entered. A wreath woven of autumn leaves, dried thistles and lacquered milkweed pods hung on it. Very attractive. But not the sort of thing a man would hang on his door. The wreath was a woman's touch, and this troubled me, for Anthony had told me that there would never be another woman in his life. How could he betray me?

Before going to my own apartment, I made a mental note of his unit number: 616.

Back in my own apartment, I made a pot of camomile tea to soothe my nerves while I sorted things out. To an ordinary, secular intelligence, it might appear that the Anthony who had visited me every night was a fantasy. Such a conclusion would be too simplistic. To be theological about it, I created Anthony the Word, while the Anthony whose picture appeared in the *Toronto Star* and who now lived in my apartment building was the Word Made Flesh. A paradox? Of course. Many a higher truth is hidden within a paradox. There were not two Anthonys. Anthony the Word and Anthony Incarnate were one and indivisible.

This was not difficult for me to understand, for I have always been able to grasp truths that lie beyond the reach of ordinary intelligence. At school, the nuns repressed me. They expelled me when I likened myself to the child Jesus in the Temple. The Vatican was behind this persecution. I know that now.

There was only one Anthony. But possibly there were two women. If such proved to be the case, one of us would have to go.

The next morning I took my binoculars from the drawer. Early light shining into the west-wing windows facing me gave me the perfect viewing opportunity. I carried a chair over to the living-room window and sat there, eating my boiled egg and toast as I waited for the drapes to open at apartment number 616, feeling fairly sure I knew which one that was.

I was finishing my toast when the drapes parted, and there in full view stood a woman wearing a pink bathrobe. After wiping my fingers on a serviette, I focused my binoculars. The woman, blond and petite, looked like the same one who had been standing beside my Anthony in the *Toronto Star* photograph.

Through the binoculars I saw Anthony, wearing a deep red dressing gown, approach her, carrying two coffee mugs. He gave her one, and they stood side by side, apparently watching the sky as they sipped from the mugs.

There was a roaring in my ears, and a stricture in my chest so that I could hardly breathe. How dare my Anthony stand by that woman's shoulder, so relaxed and easy! And then he did the most terrible thing. He kissed the top of her head. The binoculars fell from my hands and dangled on my chest by their leather strap.

When I had steadied myself enough to look again, I saw Anthony walk away. The woman, moving about, looked as if she was tidying up. She left the room. Half an hour later, she returned. Now she was wearing a skimpy blue dress that left her legs bare halfway up her thighs. Surely she didn't plan to wear that to work! Apparently, yes. In a few moments she left the room with a handbag over her shoulder.

I looked at my wristwatch. Ten past eight. Watching the events in Apartment 616, I had neither showered nor dressed. For the first time in my twenty years at Erskine Press, I was late for work.

The next morning the scene was repeated. Pink bathrobe. Red dressing gown, Two mugs of coffee. The perfunctory kiss placed on the top of the woman's head. No passion in that. However this insignificant woman had managed to entrap him, Anthony had no feeling for her now. It was my mission to free him from the shackles of a loveless marriage.

Showered and dressed, I was prepared. As before, Anthony was the first to withdraw from my field of vision. After a few minutes, the woman followed. The previous day she had taken half an hour to get ready for work. There was no need for me to hurry. I finished my cup of tea before taking the elevator to the lobby.

Standing off to one side, I waited.

The elevator went up and down several times before she stepped out, this time in a green dress. I followed at her heels. Even wearing stiletto pumps, she was half a head shorter than I. In weight I had a thirty-pound advantage.

I kept a little space between us all the way to the subway stop and was right behind her descending the stairs. When we reached the platform, I heard a roar of voices in my head, and the loudest voice of all was Anthony's: "Do it! Do it now!"

A push would not accomplish my purpose. She was too far from the edge. "Do it!" Anthony's voice filled my head. "Do it! Do it!" I rushed at her, hauled her to the brink, and hurled her onto the tracks. She screamed. Arms flailing, she landed on the middle rail one second before the train struck.

Now Anthony is with me always.

At our next session I explain to Dr. Freitag that I am greater than Jesus, who had the power to heal but not to create. "Isn't that true?" I ask her, speaking rhetorically. "Did Jesus create even one new, unique human being?"

"Not that I know of," she answers.

And then she deliberately changes the subject. I have noticed that she does this when she finds herself out of her intellectual depth.

"How is Anthony?" Dr. Freitag asks. This is a safe subject. Since learning that Anthony is with me all the time, she always asks after him. She cannot see him. No one but I can see him. He is sitting right here with us, in a chair just like the one in which I am seated. He leans back and smiles at me. It is that sweet angelic smile allowed only for me.

Dr. Freitag asks about the kind of things Anthony and I do together.

He nods while I explain how we collaborate in our work. There is a library here at Penetanguishene. I tell her that every day we take a different book from the shelves in order to check it for typos, inconsistencies, and grammatical errors. "You would be amazed," I say, "at the number we find in even the most respected publications."

Dr. Freitag tells me that she has almost finished writing her book.

"Congratulations!" I say. "Anthony and I will check your manuscript carefully before you submit it for publication."

What the Gardener Saw

The dew is still on the grass when Cec rides his bicycle around to the back of the house and leans it against the garden shed. Mrs. Lindor must be watching for him, because she comes out the French doors onto the patio before he has had time to put the lock on his bike.

She is wearing tight pants and a tight pink T-shirt with a neck so low he can look right down her boobs. She knows he can, but she doesn't care. Her gaze slides over him as if he wasn't there.

"This morning you can dig up the peonies and move them to the flower bed by the fence, where they'll get more sun. After that, you can mow the lawn."

Mrs. Lindor never says "Good morning," or "How are you?" and certainly not "Please." She is a stuck-up bitch. If he looks at her with half-closed eyes, she reminds him of Miss Parks, his Grade 7 teacher, the one who told him to sit at the back of the room and keep quiet if he couldn't learn anything. He was fourteen years old in Grade Seven. Miss Parks had pointy breasts like two cones. Sitting there in his seat in the back row, he used to wonder what her boobs would feel like if he squeezed them. Like rubber, maybe?

Miss Parks treated him like a piece of shit. That's the same way Mrs. Lindor treats him. She is a real looker, with blond hair in different shades that hangs in layers to her shoulders. Her eyes are blue, with long, thick lashes. What he likes best about her are her boobs and her ass. Mrs. Lindor looks about thirty, but Cec figures she has to be older.

As she gives him his orders, she is standing so close that he can smell her. Like roses, but not quite. As she turns away, he wants to grab the flesh of her bum in one hand and pinch. He watches her ass, enjoying the way her cheeks move up and down, as she walks across the flagstone patio back into the house.

Cec comes once a week, on Wednesdays, to mow the Lindors' lawn and work in their garden. Once – only once – he has felt the touch of Mrs. Lindor's fingers as she handed him his pay. Her fingernails are dark red, with little pictures painted on them. His fingernails are dirty. The time she touched his hand, he was sure she did it on purpose. She was teasing him, just like she teases her lover.

A couple of times, Cec nearly phoned Mr. Lindor at his office to tell him about the lover. Mr. Lindor is a lawyer in Toronto. He has grey hair and wears suits. Cec does not see him often. Mr. Lindor usually leaves for work in his shiny, black Jaguar at 6:00 a.m.

The Lindors have two children, boys in their early teens. They are away at some snooty summer camp, so they don't get in Mrs. Lindor's way. She has plenty of time to spend as she pleases.

If Cec ever makes that phone call, Mr. Lindor will put a stop to the lover. That is why Cec hasn't called. He doesn't want the affair to end. If it ends he won't be able to watch Mrs. Lindor and her lover have sex. They do it on the living room carpet, which is pale and creamy and looks very soft.

When he stands outside the dining room window, which is at the rear of the house, Cec has a good view all the way to the living room. Luckily for him, the dining room drapes don't quite meet. Cec wants to do things like the lover does with Mrs. Lindor.

The lover's name is Rob. Cec has never heard his last name. Rob has bodybuilder muscles. He wears jeans and cowboy boots, and he has a small gold ring in his ear. He drives a jeep with a licence plate that begins R O B. Cec recognizes the letters.

Cec isn't much to look at, and he knows it. Beanpole is what people call him. His arms are long, and his left shoulder is higher than his right. His mouth is wide, with no lips, and he has a huge Adam's apple. He is forty-eight years old and has never had sex with a woman.

While Cec is digging the hole for the peonies, he hears a car approaching. Looking up, he sees Rob's jeep. Nothing unusual about that. Rob is apt to show up any time that Mr. Lindor isn't home.

But the jeep is going too fast. There is a metre-deep ditch alongside the road, with a culvert under the entrance to the driveway. The jeep's brakes squeal as the jeep slows for the turn, and it barely misses the ditch. Cec leans on his spade, watching. If the jeep went into the ditch, they'd have to call a tow truck to pull it out.

The jeep brakes with a spray of gravel. Rob steps out, slams the door, and marches up to the house. Just as if he owned the place, he opens the front door and disappears inside.

What the hell? Cec scratches his head. Something must be up. Rob always rings the bell and waits for Mrs. Lindor to let him in. Why not this time?

With the windows closed, Cec can't hear what is going on inside the house. Shouldering the spade, he saunters over to the shrubbery under the dining room window, trying to look as if he has something to do over there.

Through the gap in the drapes he sees Mrs. Lindor and Rob facing each other, circling like a pair of fighters ready to throw the first punch. They hurl their words like weapons. Cec cannot hear everything, but he hears enough to figure out that Rob wants money and Mrs. Lindor won't give him any. She says he is de-spittable. She tells him that she's tired of him and snaps her fingers right in front of his eyes. He calls her a whore, slaps her, and strides from the room.

Cec pulls back from the window. Without appearing to hurry, he returns to the flower bed with the spade over his shoulder. When Rob bursts out of the house, Cec already has his spade in the earth. He pushes the blade hard into the soil; that helps to control his shaking.

At lunchtime Cec sits behind the garden shed and eats a ham and cheese sandwich that he bought, ready-made, at Tim Hortons on his way to work. With it, he drinks a can of Coca-Cola. By leaving his plastic-wrapped sandwich under a clay flowerpot with a wet burlap sack on top, he keeps it cool. Some employers let him put his lunch in their fridge, but not Mrs. Lindor.

He sits next to the compost pile, which is mostly grass clippings, with his back resting against the wall of the shed and his legs stretched out. The chipmunk that lives behind the shed has popped out of its hole and sits up on its hind legs, looking at him. The chipmunk is so close he can see a flea run through the white hairs on its belly. While he munches his sandwich and watches the chipmunk, he is thinking about Mrs. Lindor.

Has Rob done something bad to her? Cec can find out easily by knocking at the back door. When she answers, he can ask to use the basement washroom. Not even Mrs. Lindor denies him the use of a toilet. But the silence of the house unsettles him, even though he is sure she has come to no serious harm. It was just a slap, after all. He smiles as he remembers the sharp smack of Rob's palm against her cheek and the way her eyes flew open with astonishment and pain. Somebody ought to slap her more often. He holds up his right hand, with its dirty fingernails and grimy knuckles. He wouldn't mind giving her a slap like that. His senses tingle at the thought of it. His calloused palm. Her soft cheek.

After finishing his lunch, he urinates on the compost pile.

The Lindors' house has an acre of lawn. He makes the first cut using their John Deere garden tractor, and then finishes around the shrubberies and flower beds with the Gardena reel mower. Grass-cutting takes him the whole afternoon.

At six o'clock, his work finished and the garden machinery and tools back in the shed, Cec approaches the French doors and knocks. He'll act normal, he decides, as if he knew nothing about the slap and Rob storming out of the house. He always collects his one hundred dollars for the day's work before leaving.

Through the French doors he sees Mrs. Lindor walking toward him. She is still wearing those tight pants and that tight pink T-shirt that shows off her boobs. Her face is perfect. No sign of tears. Opening one of the French doors, she steps outside. Now, in the clear light, he sees the red mark on her left cheek where Rob slapped her.

"I'm sorry, but you'll have to wait until next week for your pay …" She raises her eyes to meet his. "Unless you'll take a cheque." A pause. "I'm short of cash. I couldn't go to the bank today because my car won't start. The garage is sending a man tomorrow to take a look."

"I can wait for Mr. Lindor to come home."

"He'll be late." She pouts her lower lip. "He has to stay in the city for a meeting. I don't expect him much before midnight." Another pause. "Are you sure you won't accept a cheque?"

"Has to be cash." He can't admit to her that he does not have a bank account, so a personal cheque would be no good to him. Cec shifts his weight from one foot to the other. "You can pay me next week."

"Well, it's up to you."

Her voice is unsteady. Suddenly she seems unsure of herself. Short of cash. Car broken down. Fight with her lover. Home alone.

He feels the balance between them shift. Cec is the one in control. In less time than needed to take one breath, the thought comes to him. *She can't stop me. I can do anything I want.* He stands staring at her, his hands making fists.

She steps backwards quickly. "Then I'll pay you next week."

Mrs. Lindor retreats into the house, her cute ass pushing against the fabric of her tight slacks. The door closes. Cec watches through the glass as she walks away into the safety of her three-million-dollar home. He feels his cock spring up in his pants. She's asking for it, with that sexy walk and her tight T-shirt. He should tell her what he has seen her do with Rob. He squeezes his fingernails into his palms. Stuck-up bitch! Who does she think she is?

What would happen if he pounded on the door? Probably she would come to ask what he wanted. When he told her, she'd tell him to fuck off. No, she wouldn't say that. She didn't talk that way. Maybe she'd threaten to tell her husband. He hoped she would. Then he could say to her, "Go ahead. I'll tell him about your boyfriend screwing you on the living room floor."

Cec raises his fist to pound on the door. Then he loses his nerve. His erection wilts as he heads toward the garden shed to get his bike.

Pedalling down the long driveway, he feels Mrs. Lindor's eyes on him. Or maybe that is his imagination. Why would she be looking at him – a skinny man in dirty jeans? Not even a man, in her eyes. Doesn't own a car.

"Costs too much," he always says whenever a customer suggests he buy a pickup truck. He could look after twice as many lawns and gardens if he had a vehicle. He could carry his own lawn mower and tools and charge more. Cec knows all that.

His secret – and he has never breathed it to a soul – is that he cannot read. And since he cannot read, he could not study the manual that they hand out at the Motor Licensing Bureau. Nor could he write the written part of the driving exam. If he couldn't learn to read or write during all the years he went to school, there is no way he could learn that stuff now.

At the end of the driveway, Cec turns right onto the sideroad, riding between farmers' fields where the corn is shoulder-high. Run-off water from all the rain they had in July stands in the ditches that flank the road.

The Lindors live in Flamborough, on acreage that was a working farm ten years ago. They had the old farmhouse and outbuildings torn down to make way for their big, fancy house. It is a stone house, two storeys high. Maybe in one hundred years it will look as if it belongs there. Right now it looks stupid, with those skinny ten-foot poplars edging the driveway.

He had worked for the Lindors before they moved out of town. If it weren't to see Mrs. Lindor, he probably wouldn't spend twenty minutes coming out here and twenty minutes going back every week. None of his other customers lives in the country. He does the yardwork for six different properties. Four of his customers are old ladies. Apart from Mrs. Lindor, the only good-looker is Mrs. Gould, his Thursday client. She is a Jewish lady with pink cheeks, brown eyes, and dark, wavy hair. She always asks him how he is, and she says please and thank you. She lets him keep his lunch in her refrigerator. On hot days she brings him a glass of iced tea and sometimes sits beside him on the garden bench while he drinks it. Mrs. Gould smiles a lot and waves her hands around while she talks. She is the exact opposite of the cold and snooty Mrs. Lindor.

With the ten dollars he has in his pocket, he has enough to buy a hamburger on his way back to the rooming house where he lives. He's not broke. But it irks him that he has not been paid. What if Mrs. Lindor forgets about it? What if she says next week that she already paid him? It will be her word against his. He keeps on pedalling while he thinks about this. If he wants to be sure of that hundred bucks he is owed, he had better go back and wait for Mr. Lindor to come home.

At the intersection of the sideroad and Concession 2 there is a service station with a diner. He'll stop there for a hamburger, he decides, and then go back to the Lindors' house.

When he reaches the service station, there is one car at the gas pumps. It pulls away while he is sliding his bike into the rack by the door. Inside, he is the only customer. Cec orders a hamburger and sits down at a small Arborite-topped table. From the far side of the half-door to the kitchen come the sizzle and the smell of his hamburger on the grill.

They make good burgers at this place, with home fries on the side. Cec is hungrier than he expected to be. As he chows down on the food, he feels like a warrior preparing for battle. Mrs. Lindor will be surprised to see him. Maybe he'll give her a special surprise, if he doesn't lose his nerve.

He pays for his hamburger. It's a ten-minute ride back to the Lindor place, and all the way he thinks about Mrs. Lindor. What is she doing now? Eating dinner? Watching TV? Painting her fingernails? He ought to barge right in, the way Rob did that morning. Then she'd know he meant business. Exactly what he would do after barging in, he is not sure. He will have to play it by ear.

The idea of hiding his bicycle in the ditch comes to him just after he has turned off Concession 2 and started north on the sideroad. It might be smart to go the last mile on foot. Then, if a car comes along, he can quickly step off the pavement, either into the ditch or behind a bush. Depending on what happens later between him and Mrs. Lindor, he may not want anybody to have seen him riding his bike toward the Lindor place, or away.

The ditch is a metre deep, and dry at the spot where he leaves his bicycle. Cec does not lock it. Maybe he'll be in a hurry later on. The sun is setting, and mist rising. His bike will be safe.

As he nears the Lindors' property, he feels a moment of fear that Rob will be there. He might have returned to apologize and make up, although it isn't likely, Cec thinks, that Mrs. Lindor would want him back. Still, Cec is relieved to see no jeep or any other vehicle in the driveway. Mrs. Lindor is alone.

The outside entrance light shines through a haze of mist. The hanging baskets of flowers on both sides of the front door have lost their colour. Fog veils everything. It hides Cec as he scurries around to the dining room window at the back of the house. From there he can see whether Mrs. Lindor is in the living room. To watch her for a few minutes seems a smart idea.

Mrs. Lindor is sitting in an armchair, still wearing her tight pants and skinny T-shirt. Her bare feet rest on a footstool. She is reading a magazine. A cup and saucer stand on a small table beside the chair. Wouldn't she be surprised if she knew that he is watching her!

He returns to the front of the house and rings the bell. Her bare feet make no sound as she comes to the door. She must have seen him through the little round spy hole in the door, because, after a few seconds, the door opens.

"Cec? Is there a problem?"

"I need to get paid."

"But I told you –"

"I know what you told me. I'm going to wait for Mr. Lindor."

Her hand is on the door. She makes a slight move, as if she intends to close it.

"My husband may not be home for hours." With a smooth motion, she checks her watch, which is a tiny clock face set in a thick gold bracelet.

"I'll wait inside."

"No." She jumps. "I can't let you in. Not when I'm home alone." The door begins to close.

If she didn't look so scared, Cec wouldn't have the nerve to rush the door. He throws his weight against it before it reaches the jamb.

Mrs. Lindor staggers backwards, caught off balance.

"Get out!"

He almost obeys. It is second nature to do as he is told. He is scared. He wants to run away. Too late for that.

Her voice shrills. "Get out!" It rings in his ears.

Mrs. Lindor backs up against a hall table. On the table are three tall, heavy-looking china vases with pictures on them of slanty-eyed people. Mrs. Lindor is staring at him. Her eyes are wide, and the corners of her mouth pull back as though she is going to scream.

It seems to go on for a long time, this moment. Then Mrs. Lindor turns sideways. With both hands she grabs the largest vase, the one in the middle, and raises it like a club.

A blur of motion. Cec seizes her wrists. The vase crashes to the floor.

"Fuck you! Fuck you!" Cec hears himself yelling. Mrs. Lindor starts screaming. Her screams fill his head. He lets go of her wrists, grasps the vase nearest to him and smashes it into the side of her head. He strikes her again. And again.

Her body seems to fold as she drops to the floor.

Knees bent and shoulders slouched, Cec stares down at her. He feels woozy, powerless to act, as if trapped in a dream.

Mrs. Lindor's blue eyes are wide open, but they aren't looking at him. He hears a rattle in her throat. Her eyes roll back.

Cec steps backwards. The front door is wide open. He turns and runs, runs blindly into the yellow-grey fog. He has reached the end of the driveway when he sees the headlights of a car coming toward him. Its beams slice like blades of light through the mist. Cec sees enough to recognize the Jaguar's sleek form.

He jumps sideways before the headlights' beams can catch him. Suddenly the ground drops away from under his feet. The ditch. He had forgotten the ditch. Arms flailing, he stumbles to the bottom. In an instant, on his hands and knees in cold water, he feels his mind clear.

Pinpoint alert, he keeps his head down as the car slows. Gravel crunches as it turns in to the driveway. Even in fog, Mr. Lindor knows just where to turn. At the house, the car stops. The engine turns off.

"Oh, my God!" Mr. Lindor's feet pound toward the door. The mist heightens every sound.

Cec raises his head to look. From the glow of light at the entrance, he realizes that he left the front door wide open. He scrambles out of the ditch. On his clothes there will be burdock burs and juices from crushed milkweed stalks. From his hands and knees there will be an imprint in the mud under the shallow water. His shoes will leave prints. But thousands of guys wear size-ten sneakers from Zellers.

Now he is running, wet shoes squelching, slapping the asphalt. The mist makes it hard to see, but he does not slow down. He keeps on running and running. By the time he reaches the spot where he left his bike, there is a stitch in his side. The bicycle is still there. He crouches in the ditch long enough to quiet his gasping breath before wheeling his bike onto the road.

When he passes the service station at the intersection, he sees only a dim night light inside the diner. He turns east onto Concession 2. In ten minutes, he'll be home.

Cec hears the siren before he sees the lights. He jumps off the bike, pulls it into the bushes alongside the road and waits while the cop car hurtles by. An ambulance follows.

The rest of the way to town, he has the road to himself.

When Cec reaches his rooming house, he walks his bicycle into the garage, where the landlady lets him keep it. It must be midnight by now. No lights show in the windows. Everybody must be asleep.

As he crosses the yard from the garage to the back door, a bat swoops past him toward the eaves of the house. Before unlocking the door, he takes off his shoes to carry them inside.

He tries to be quiet in the bathroom. The water in the toilet bowl is yellow. Cec adds his pee. The landlady has a rule not to flush at night. It's a good rule. He does not want to disturb anyone's sleep, not tonight.

He climbs into bed. There is a rip in the bottom sheet. He did that with his big toenail last week. The landlady might make him pay for the torn sheet. She makes him pay for every little thing.

Tomorrow is Cec's day for Mrs. Gould. She's a nice lady. Always friendly. Last week she was wearing a low-cut sundress that showed her cleavage. She's asking for it, too.

On his way to Mrs. Gould's house, he'll stop at the pay phone outside Mac's Milk and call 9-1-1. "If you want to know what happened to Mrs. Lindor last night," he'll say, "look for a jeep with a licence plate that begins with R O B. The owner's name is Rob."

Payback

Carter sat in the booth closest to the door, warming his hands on his coffee mug. He would rather have met Jacob some place dark and secret. But it was too cold.

At the White Spot Grill people come and go. Carter figured he wouldn't be noticed. He was not the sort of person that attracted notice. He was a blue-eyed man with dirty-blond hair cut close. He wore glasses. He was neither tall nor short. His black leather coat was neither new nor old. He wore scuffed brown boots.

When he saw Jacob through the glass of the White Spot's door, Carter put his right hand under the table, laying it on his thigh. Probably he should have kept his right hand hidden all along. It was the only thing about him that people would notice.

Jacob Vogel opened the door and closed it quickly behind him. He was shorter than Carter, with a broad, snub-nosed face, and just as ordinary to look at.

He was wearing a windbreaker, jeans and dirty white trainers. Not dressed for winter. From the brown stubble on his cheeks and chin, he looked like he hadn't shaved for a couple of days. His eyes fixed straight ahead, he approached the booth and slid onto the bench facing Carter. Jacob's eyes were burning red, as if he had been crying. Liquor could cause the same effect. Carter smelled stale whisky on Jacob's breath.

Seeing him so close, without a glass barrier between them, Carter started to shake. Under the table, he made a fist with his right hand. Wincing at the pain, he felt a year of rage boil to the surface.

Jacob leaned forward. "I gotta get away." His voice was a hoarse whisper. "I need money."

Carter grunted. "Sorry. I can't help you there."

"You've always come through for me."

"Christ! I've been out of work for six months. I'm broke."

"You can get it for me."

"How am I supposed to do that?" Carter snorted. "Rob a bank, maybe?"

"My mom will give it to you. I've already phoned her."

"Your mom! Get real. She doesn't know me from a hole in the wall."

"I told her you're the one friend who's always stood by me." He paused. "She understands. My mom's been through plenty of bad stuff."

Carter sat there taking it all in. Here's a guy thirty years old who runs to his mommy when he gets in trouble.

"Go yourself," Carter snapped. "Why send me?"

"People might see me," Jacob whined. "Neighbours know who I am. Look, I'll give you her address. She lives on Mill Street East, about four blocks from here. Get the money. Then we'll meet."

Without waiting for an answer, Jacob pulled from his jacket pocket a ballpoint pen and a crumpled cash register receipt.

"What makes you think she'll have money in the house?" Carter asked. "I mean, serious money. Fifty bucks won't get you far."

"She doesn't trust banks," Jacob said as he scribbled an address on the back of the receipt.

"How much is she good for?"

"Couldn't say. Money's her big secret. She hides it different places. Russians looted her house during the Occupation."

"What occupation?"

"After World War II. In Germany."

"You never told me your folks were from Germany."

"Didn't I? My father was a *Panzerjäger.*"

"A what?"

"He knocked out tanks." Jacob's mouth twisted in a bitter smile. "Heil Hitler!"

"Your father still alive?"

"No, no. He died years ago. Heart attack. My mother lives alone … alone with her saints and my father's army souvenirs." Jacob pushed the paper across the table to Carter. "I knew I could count on you." The paper lay on the table between them. Carter leaned forward, squinting at the address.

He flexed his fingers under the table. Two years after the accident, sharp twinges reminded him that his little finger and ring finger were gone. Whenever he felt the pain, he would flex his remaining fingers. It helped.

"If I do this … after I get the money, where will I find you?"

"Right here."

"The sign on the door says the White Spot closes at ten. It's nine already."

"Then bring it to the place I'm hiding."

"Where's that?"

"Five or six blocks from here. It's an abandoned garage in the alley that runs through the block between Odessa Street and Raglan Road."

"Is it safe?"

"Nobody ever goes there. Not in winter."

"Maybe I can't find it. I don't know this part of town."

Jacob frowned. "You can find it. Go two blocks east along Main –"

"I'll walk there with you now. I need to be sure." Carter tried to keep his voice steady, steeling himself. Using his left hand, he picked up the receipt bearing Mrs. Vogel's address. As he shoved the scrap of paper into his coat pocket, his fingers brushed the knife. At the counter, Carter paid for his coffee. He had just enough cash for that. Tomorrow he'd be eating steak.

On the sidewalk, Jacob walked bent over, hugging himself for warmth. Wind-driven grains of snow lashed both their faces. The temperature was –20 Celsius. It must be freezing in that garage, Carter thought.

It had been cold like this the night it happened. Jacob driving drunk. The car rolling. Carter pinned by his hand.

Sandi, Carter's girl, crushed under the car. All Carter could see of her were her boots with the three-inch heels, and her crimson blood staining the white snow.

"We saved your hand," the doctor told him. "You're lucky you lost only two fingers."

"I lost my girlfriend," Carter said.

The doctor looked embarrassed to have been so clumsy. "I'm sorry," he said.

Every time Carter felt the phantom pain where his missing fingers had been, he felt the pain of his greater loss. Sometimes he deliberately made a hard fist so he could feel that pain. It helped him to remember Sandi – the clean smell of her shiny hair and the silky softness of her skin.

Jacob escaped with a few bruises and one year in jail. Drunk driving. Motor manslaugter.

"I don't blame you," Carter told Jacob on his first visit to the jail. "It could happen to anybody."

Jacob wiped his eyes with the back of his hand. "I wouldn't blame you if you hated me."

Carter hid the truth.

In the first weeks, he had felt nothing but pain and grief. But pain turned to anger and grief to rage. How do you kill a guy who's behind bars? You don't. You have to wait. So Carter had waited. Every time he had visited Jacob, he had thought how it would be. An eye for an eye, like the Bible said. That would put things right.

And then, this afternoon, one week out of jail, Jacob did it again. Drunk. Stolen car. Young kid trudging home from school through the snow. Probably with one of those twenty-pound backpacks they all wear. You can't jump out of the way with something that heavy weighing you down.

Jacob didn't want to be sent back to prison. Well, he wasn't going to be. Carter had the knife in his pocket, a clasp knife with a guard to hold open the blade. He'd bought it just for Jacob that very afternoon.

In the garage, out of the wind, it felt warmer. The window – four panes of dirty glass – gave Carter just enough light to see what he was doing.

Since losing the two fingers, his right hand did not have the grip it once had. He knew that. But he was clumsy with his left. Pulling the knife from his pocket, he switched it to his right hand, ended up using both hands to strengthen his grip. *Okay,* he said to himself. *This one's for Sandi.*

The knife entered Jacob's back horizontally. It was a good, sharp knife with a narrow blade. It encountered no bone. There was not a great deal of blood. Carter pulled out the blade. After wiping it on Jacob's pant leg, he closed the knife and shoved it into his coat pocket.

Jacob had not screamed. A gurgling sound came from him as he collapsed. Then there was quiet. The only movement was the jerking of his limbs. It lasted only a minute. Jacob lay still, his cheek on the garage floor, one arm under his body and the other reaching forward as if he had been grasping for something when he died.

Carter pulled Jacob's wallet from his pants' pocket. No bills. Just a few coins. Better take the wallet, though. It would give Carter some needed extra time if the cops required a few days to establish Jacob's ID. Even in winter, somebody might find the body.

Ten minutes later, Carter was walking east on Mill Street. Under a street light he stopped and reached into his pocket for the scrap of paper with Mrs. Vogel's address. Holding the paper close to his glasses, he compared the number with the number under the light by the front door. He took the five steps up to the front porch, stomped on the sisal mat to knock the snow off his boots, and rang the bell.

The hall light came on. Through the frosted glass panel beside the door he saw a shape shuffling toward him. He thrust the paper back into his pocket. Mrs. Vogel did not open the door at once.

"Yes?" she demanded through the glass.

"I'm Carter."

"Jacob's friend?"

"Yes."

She opened the door. Carter stepped inside. Instantly his glasses misted. He could see nothing.

"Take off your coat."

"No. I'm not staying." But he removed his gloves.

With his left hand, he pulled off his glasses and shoved them into his coat pocket. He could see well enough without them, at least well enough to see the broad cheeks and snub nose of the woman who stood in front of him. She was in her sixties, a dumpy woman in a shapeless black dress, with thin, greying hair pulled into a tight knot at the back of her head. At the wide part in her hair, her scalp was yellow. Carter was not tall, just five-foot-nine. Yet the woman facing him came barely to his shoulder

"Come in, anyway," she said. "It's drafty in the front hall." Her English was clear, despite her German accent.

As Carter followed her down the narrow hallway, she asked over her shoulder if Jacob would soon be home.

"That's not something I can tell you, Mrs. Vogel. Jake's in trouble."

"So what's new?"

She led him into a small sitting room dominated by a white marble fireplace that must have been the homeowner's pride when the house was built ... maybe a hundred years ago. A crack ran diagonally from the right side just under the mantel to the firebox opening.

Carter waited for the woman to take a seat before saying more. She settled into a deep armchair. He did not sit down.

"There's been an accident," he said. "Jake was driving."

"Is he all right?"

"Yeah, but he hit a kid, a boy about ten. The kid was walking along the side of the road."

"At night?"

"No. Four this afternoon."

"Where did this happen?"

"Right outside Kilbride, maybe a quarter mile from the village. Jake told me he wanted to stop. He would have stopped." Carter shrugged. "Look. He knew he'd fail the Breathalyzer test. So he kept going." Carter shifted his gaze away from the woman's face.

"Is the boy hurt bad?"

"He's dead. It was on the six o'clock news. His father went looking for him when he wasn't home in time for supper. He found his son in the ditch, still alive. He died on the way to hospital. The report said he might have survived if he'd got medical attention right away."

Mrs. Vogel pressed her lips into a straight line. She inhaled sharply, then let out her breath. "Jacob must turn himself in."

"Look. Jake is hiding. He can't turn himself in. This isn't a first offence, you know." Carter felt the twinges again. This time he pulled his hand out of his pocket, flexed his index and middle fingers.

Mrs. Vogel saw his hand. She looked away.

"Jake told me he'd never go back inside," Carter said. "Not one more night in the cells. If the police arrest him, they'll charge him with motor manslaughter, plus leaving the scene of an accident. Jake has to get away. He needs cash."

She shook her head. "Tell him no. I can't turn him in. I'm his mother. But he gets no help from me."

"He's counting on you," Carter said. "He told me you'd give him money." Carter's left hand reached into his coat pocket, closed around the clasp knife. When she saw the knife, saw the blade snap open, Mrs. Vogel's face went pale.

"Oh!" she said. "Did Jacob tell you to threaten me?"

"He said to do whatever it took."

Both hands grasping the arms of her chair, she hauled herself to her feet. "I'll get my purse."

He followed her upstairs to a bedroom that was stuffed with dark furniture. Her black leather handbag lay on the heavy quilt that covered the bed. She opened her purse and pulled out a wallet. "Here," she said as she handed him a few bills. "That's all I have in the house."

"There's more. Jake told me."

Carter raised his hand that held the knife, bringing it level with Mrs. Vogel's jugular. She stared at the narrow blade.

"*Gott in Himmel.*" Her breath caught. "*Es gibt Blut.*"

"Shut up with your Kraut gibberish," Carter said. "Hurry up and get me the money."

Carter looked around the room. Hanging on a nail beside a framed print of the Bleeding Heart of Mary was a silver crucifix. Worth something. But it might be hard to fence.

Mrs. Vogel was shaking so hard Carter thought she might collapse right there in front of him. Her eyes were fixed on the knife. When he flicked a glance at the blade, he saw the stain of blood. Damn! Had she noticed? Would he have to kill her too?

"Get me the money," he repeated. "Jake's waiting."

"It's here. In a space under …"

She tottered unsteadily to the cast-metal heat register set into the baseboard. Peering at it, Carter saw that the screw that should have secured the grating to the frame was missing. With a grunt, Mrs. Vogel lowered herself to her knees. She lifted off the grating and laid it on the floor beside her. Bending her head, she reached her hand inside the open register. Her breathing was noisy, a wheezing sound. Her head turned toward him.

The last thing Carter saw was the flash from the Luger's muzzle.

An Afternoon at the Cottage

"Wow!" Terry said. "So this is where you disappear to on weekends."

Davey stood watching, amused, as she walked around the great room, staring up at the tongue-in-groove cathedral ceiling, down at the pine-plank floor, and through the huge picture window at the sparkling blue water of Cranberry Lake.

Terry Loucks was one of the secretaries at Strathcona Secondary School, where Davey Sturmont taught biology. She was a pretty brunette with long black hair and olive skin. For this afternoon at the cottage, she was wearing a ski sweater and slacks. At thirty, Terry had been married once and would like to be married again, preferably to Davey. But he already had a wife.

On that same afternoon, Davey's wife Sue and their two little girls were in Toronto, enjoying a Saturday matinee performance of *The Lion King,* thus providing Davey with an opportunity to bring Terry to the cottage. Terry did not like motels. For her, this would be a treat.

While Terry roamed about saying "Wow!" at everything in sight, Davey turned on the electric baseboard heating. This was the first weekend of October, and the cottage had been closed up since the previous Sunday.

Terry, standing on the thick sheepskin rug that lay in front of the massive stone fireplace, turned to Davey.

"May I have a tour?"

"Of course." He had looked forward to showing off his summer home.

With a wave he directed her toward the kitchen, which was open to the great room. Following her, he could not help grinning at the way she stared about.

"Wow! You have way more appliances in this cottage than I have in my whole apartment. Stove. Fridge. Washer. Dryer. Dishwasher. Indoor grill. Microwave. Talk about taking life easy!"

Her enthusiasm pleased him.

"My mother-in-law was responsible for most of the upgrades. She didn't like roughing it. The only way she would come up to the cottage was if she could have every convenience of her house in town. The microwave is the only thing Sue has added since she took over."

"So it's your wife's cottage, really?"

He flinched. "It's our family cottage. But yes, she holds title."

"Nice to have money."

Davey did not answer. It riled him that it was Sue who had the money. What riled him even more was her persistence in ignoring his hints that the deed should be changed to joint ownership. He would have appreciated survivorship rights. Not only that, but Sue's sole owner-ship sometimes made him feel more like a guest at the cottage than lord of the manor.

Terry, her elbows resting on the granite counter, gazed out the window at Cranberry Lake sparkling in the sunshine. "I can just imagine standing here peeling potatoes while enjoying that view."

The autumn colours were at their height: crimson, russet, yellow and gold.

"Fall is my favourite season," he said. "I wanted to share this with you."

"Look!" she exclaimed. "Two people out in a canoe."

He glanced in the direction she pointed. "Yeah. I see them. No life jackets."

In the stern of a red canoe knelt a big, sandy-haired man wearing a tan windbreaker. The woman, paddling in the bow, had her brown hair in a ponytail. She wore a black backpack over her blue jacket.

"I know the guy," Davey said. "Alvin Tofflemire. The Tofflemires' cottage is further up the lake from here. I don't know the girl." He snickered. "Looks like Al is having a bit on the side. Everybody's doing it."

"Let's have the rest of the tour," Terry said stiffly.

From the great room, a short corridor led to the bedrooms. The door to the first one stood open.

"This is Kate's room."

"She's four, isn't she?"

"Can't you tell?"

A laminated circus poster dominated one plank wall. On the bed cushions were piles of stuffed animals. Picture books lined the shelves.

"Sweet," Terry said.

Next came eight-year-old Sally's room, where framed pictures of dogs decorated the walls. As well as books about dogs, the shelves held a collection of china dogs, each representing a different breed.

"I guess Sally likes dogs," Terry said.

"Crazy about them."

"Does she have one?"

"No. Sue won't allow an animal in the house." He chuckled. "She barely tolerates me."

"The animal in you is what I like best."

"Grr." He took a playful nip at her ear.

"Ouch! Stop that!"

Davey liked to think of himself as tough and slightly threatening. In fact, he was a soft man, not in good shape, at thirty-seven already developing a paunch. He had a broad face with regular features, and reddish-brown hair in a buzz cut, which he considered youthful and athletic.

Terry smiled and rubbed her ear. "Now show me the master bedroom."

"This way."

She stopped at the next door. "Here?"

"No. That's a bathroom."

At the end of the hall he opened the door to a spacious room with its own fireplace. A deep blue Persian carpet with red and yellow medallions covered half the floor. The window drapes and the king-size bed's quilted comforter picked up the carpet's jewel-like tones.

"Wow! This is bigger than my whole apartment." She strolled about, peering into the two walk-in closets and inspecting the ensuite with its Jacuzzi tub. When she had finished looking around, she sat down on the edge of the bed, kicked off her shoes, and lay back. "I want to try this out." She folded her arms behind her head and smiled an invitation.

Davey moved toward her, then stopped.

"Uh-uh. Not here."

"Why not?"

"Sue and I …" Davey faltered. This was not a good time to tell his girlfriend that he loved and honoured his wife.

"Some things are sacred. Right?"

He flushed. "There are things it doesn't seem right to share."

"Well, okay." She sat up. "But I notice you don't mind sharing your pecker."

He laughed. "The cottage may be Sue's, but the pecker is mine."

Terry's smile seemed forced. "All right. So which bedroom do we use? Where do you put your guests?"

"We could use a guest room, but what I had in mind was the sheepskin on the hearth in the great room. I can light a fire."

She was putting on her shoes. "Sounds romantic. We can share a bottle of wine."

"I forgot to bring any."

"What about the wine I saw in the kitchen?"

"Sue would notice a bottle missing. We never keep more than a few on hand. Kids from the trailer park outside Seeley's Bay sometimes break into cottages. If they find enough alcohol to get drunk, they trash the place."

Terry frowned. Davey did not blame her. Sharing a bottle of wine was something they both liked to do when they made love.

"Come on," he said, and guided her back to the great room. "You relax while I light a fire."

Terry settled in an armchair while he arranged paper, kindling and logs. He had done this a hundred times before, but when he had lit the fire, the logs refused to catch. After a lovely flare while the paper and kindling burned, the flames died.

"I'll try again." Davey felt inept. He had wanted to impress Terry.

"It doesn't matter. I'm not cold."

She slipped from the chair and crossed to the hearth, where she knelt beside him on the thick, warm sheepskin. With a smile, she pulled off her sweater and unhooked her brassiere. Then she leaned toward him and pressed her mouth to his. He did not respond. His body felt awkward and stiff.

Again she kissed him, pushing her tongue into his mouth. A little aroused, he placed one hand upon her round, smooth breast and leaned her backwards upon the rug. Still he felt no tightening in his groin. He wanted his penis to become huge and hard. Nothing happened.

"What's wrong?" she asked.

"I don't know. Put your clothes on. Let's go to a motel."

The absurdity struck him. Why had he brought Terry here? Invading Sue's domain, he couldn't help comparing Terry to Sue. How had he got himself into this affair with a woman who didn't have half his wife's brains or class? If Sue knew about it, she would kick him out. No more marriage. No more summers at the cottage. He would lose his children too. Terry would expect him to marry her …

Terry sat up and put on her brassiere.

"You've acted weird ever since we got here," she said.

"Sorry."

She stood up. "I'm going to the bathroom to comb my hair."

"Don't get any on the floor."

"What?"

"I don't want Sue picking up a long black hair from the bathroom floor and wondering who that belonged to."

"You make me feel cheap."

That was the way he felt too. But before he could summon a response that he would not regret, Terry had crossed the room and was looking out the window at the lake.

"There's your friend paddling back. But he's alone in the canoe."

Davey joined her at the window. "When they went by earlier, I thought they were just out for a paddle. I guess I was wrong. The girl was probably a guest, and Al was taking her over to Seeley's Bay to catch the bus. No hanky-panky after all. Well, I never did think of Al as a ladies' man." He turned from the window. "Let's get out of here."

Terry looked flustered, "First, couldn't we have a cup of tea?"

"Sorry, Honey. I'd rather not. The less we touch, the less evidence we leave. I don't want Sue to suspect that I've brought a woman up here. To her, this place is the Garden of Eden."

"So that makes me the serpent?"

"Sweetheart, you're the apple."

She giggled. And when he pretended to bite her cheek, she wrapped her arms around him. He felt a surge of relief that the crisis had passed. As she kissed his mouth, he felt his penis thickening, pushing up against his briefs.

"Come on. Let's find a motel."

The next weekend Davey, Sue and the girls drove up to Cranberry Lake to spend Thanksgiving at the cottage, as they did every year. On Sunday, while Davey took the chainsaw to a white pine that had blown down in a windstorm, Sue prepared the traditional dinner: turkey with cranberry sauce (wild, high bush cranberries that Kate and Sally had gathered), carrots, mashed potatoes and apple pie.

Alvin and Lisa Tofflemire paddled over for dinner. They were about the same age as Davey and Sue, but had no children. Although the two couples saw each other often during the summer, Thanksgiving was the only time they got together in the off-season, since the Sturmonts' home was in Kingston while the Tofflemires lived in Ottawa.

After Kate and Sally had gone to bed, the adults sipped brandy in front of a warm fire. (This time it lit properly.) Davey thought that Sue's ash-blond hair looked pretty in the firelight. She was in every way an attractive woman, long-limbed and graceful. They had met as undergraduates at Queen's University, and Davey had been smitten even before he knew about the money. It was not until she took him home to "meet the folks" that Davey realized Sue's parents were totally loaded. When she had said that she would marry him, Davey knew how lucky he was in every way.

"Have you used your cottage since the end of summer?" Sue asked the Tofflemires. The question was just to make conversation.

"This is the first visit for me since Labour Day," Lisa said. "But Al was up last weekend with a bunch of friends he knew from university." She smiled fondly at her husband. "I'm so proud of him. Those guys left the cottage neat as a pin. You'd never think that eight men had been up here fishing the weekend before."

Davey glanced from the corner of his eye at Alvin, whose smile seemed forced. Aha! Davey thought. *I was right the first time.* Although he seldom felt guilty about his own infidelity, he found it reassuring not to be the only sinner. Who could blame Al for having a girlfriend on the side? Lisa was a good woman, but she had teeth like a horse and a laugh to match. As long as she did not know, where was the harm?

On November 10th, duck hunters found the body of a woman in shallow water near the shore on the west side of Cranberry Lake. The deceased had brown hair and wore a blue jacket. The corpse was not in good shape. According to the coroner's report, it had been in the water for about one month. The lungs were filled with water. Death was by drowning, but there had also been a blow to the base of the skull, possibly inflicted by the edge of a paddle blade. Foul play was suspected.

According to news reports, the dead woman's husband, Robert Lovitt, had identified the remains. The deceased was April Lovitt, age 26, of Ottawa. She had told her husband that she was going to Sarnia to visit her sister the weekend of October 2nd to 4th. When she did not return as expected, he had phoned the sister, who informed him that no such visit had ever been planned. Mr. Lovitt had not reported his wife as a missing person. This omission was partly due to embarrassment; for he assumed that she had left him for another man. He had also hoped that she would return of her own volition.

From the day that the body was found, fear ruled Davey's life. What if Terry connected the victim with the woman they both had seen in Alvin Tofflemire's canoe? What if, after making the connection, Terry decided to tell the police? Then surely it would become public knowledge that Terry had been with Davey at the cottage that day.

Davey and Terry had not been together since that afternoon, when they had gone to a motel after fleeing the cottage. There had been no quarrel, yet in Davey's mind the affair was over. In his extramarital relationships, Davey always knew the precise moment when it was time to walk away. He had intended to tell Terry as soon as he could think of an adroit way to handle the situation. So far, he had simply avoided her. Each morning, when he arrived at the school at 8:00 a.m., he would check his pigeonhole for messages and then scurry to the science room to set up for his first class.

The discovery of the body brought his situation into sharp focus. He loved Sue. He loved Kate and Sally. He loved the cottage, and his BMW, and skiing at Whistler, and all the other luxuries that a teacher's salary could not provide. He did not love Terry. Yet if matters turned out badly, his affair with her could cost him everything else.

He wanted to tell Terry that it was time for both of them to move on. But hell hath no fury like a woman scorned. If he dumped Terry, he would have no leverage to keep her from telling the police that she had seen a man identified as Al Tofflemire, in a canoe with a woman wearing a blue jacket, paddling south on Cranberry Lake, and then the same man returning alone one hour later. If Terry went to the police with this story, Davey's name would be dragged in. Sue could put two and two together. He must not let that happen. For the foreseeable future, he would have to string Terry along.

That evening, he phoned her from the pay phone at the VIA station, which was a few miles out of town and the safest place from which to make a call.

"Sweetheart, we have to talk about what we saw that afternoon on Cranberry Lake."

"You mean, your neighbour, that girl, and the canoe?"

"Exactly. It mustn't get out that you and I were at the cottage. Besides, I've known Al Tofflemire for years. He wouldn't hurt a fly."

"We aren't talking about a fly. That was a woman."

"Maybe not the same woman."

"It looks like it happened that same weekend. She wore a blue jacket. The coroner said a paddle could have caused that injury to the base of her skull."

"Sure, sure. Anything's possible. I'm just asking you not to talk about it to anyone, especially not the police. Don't cause trouble when it isn't necessary. If Sue finds out about you and me, she'll kick me out. Not only that, but I could lose my job. You could lose yours too. You know how this Board of Education feels about improper behaviour. Please, Terry, if you and I have any chance of a future together …"

That did it.

"Davey Honey, what do you want me to do?"

Slowly he let out his breath. "Sweetheart, there's nothing for you and me to do except say nothing and be good to each other."

"I thought you were avoiding me. You haven't called me. At school, you act like I'm invisible. But you always have. I guess that's necessary."

"Now more than ever. But I want to see you. When may I come over? Tomorrow evening? I can tell Sue I have a meeting."

"Yes. Tomorrow." He heard her sigh. "Davey, I need you."

"And I need you."

What a bastard I've turned out to be, he thought as he hung up the phone.

Terry's apartment was upstairs over a hairdresser's salon in a down-at-the-heels part of town. As usual, Davey parked on a side street and waited until no pedestrians were in sight before approaching the door. It was a narrow door, painted blue, on street level. He used the key that she had given him when their affair began six months ago, and he climbed the steep staircase to the landing, where a second door opened to her apartment. He knocked. Immediately, she let him in.

There was a constant smell of cleaning products in Terry's apartment. This odour, which he found pleasant, might have been the result of Terry's constant effort to fight grime. Or it might have been the scent of shampoos from the salon below.

The apartment consisted of a small lounge, furnished with a sofa and chair in matching flowered slipcovers, a kitchenette, a bathroom with a worn claw-footed tub which a metal rod and plastic curtains had adapted for showering, and a bedroom the size of Sue's clothes closet. Davey had never liked to visit Terry here, preferring motels. But the apartment was safer. At night, there was never anyone else in the building.

Davey had brought a bottle of white wine. They made love on top of the worn chenille coverlet of her narrow bed. Before leaving, he gave her a bracelet: moonstones set in silver.

The next day, Davey noticed her wearing the bracelet at work. Two hundred dollars was a cheap price to pay for peace of mind. Everything was going to work out fine, he told himself. The police would conduct their investigation. Either they would make an arrest or they would not. He hoped that their investigation would not lead them to Alvin Tofflemire. But even if it did, Davey would be safely out of the way.

Maybe he should apply to change schools next September. Then his affair with Terry could wither away. Out of sight, out of mind. One good thing about Terry, she had a tender heart where children were involved. As for himself, once he had extricated himself, he would never be unfaithful to Sue again.

Weeks passed with no arrest. Christmas approached. Davey was beginning to feel complacent until, on the Saturday that he took Kate to see Santa Claus, his world threatened to explode.

The morning had begun well. For the first time, Kate did not wail when placed on the knee of the bearded stranger in the red snowsuit. Shyly but clearly, she confided that she wanted a princess doll and a bicycle with training wheels. Catching a nod from Davey, Santa promised to deliver.

On their way home, Davey turned on the car radio to catch the 11:00 a.m. news. That was when he learned that an arrest had been made. Kate, in the back seat, was singing "Jingle Bells." He turned up the volume to catch the name of the person charged. It was not Alvin Tofflemire.

The police had arrested somebody called Jason Giddy, of Seeley's Bay. More details would be available on the main newscast at noon.

Davey pulled into the driveway, opened the rear passenger door, and unbuckled Kate. When he lifted her from the seat, she protested indignantly, "I can walk, Daddy!" But he carried her into the house anyway, setting her down only to open the front door. In the hall, he unwound her muffler and knelt to pull off her pink boots.

"I'm making hot chocolate," Sue called from the kitchen. Davey and Kate joined her. Sally was already there, sitting at the table munching a cookie. "How was the visit to Santa?" Sue asked.

"Fine. Just fine." He left it to Kate to relate the details. Standing by the counter, listening to her little-girl chatter, he thought how much he loved her and also Sally, who, too old for Santa Claus but under orders to say nothing that would undermine her little sister's faith, wore that smug I-know-something-that-you-don't smile that is the essence of older-sisterness.

It was one minute before noon when Kate finished her story.

"I'm going to turn on the TV," Davey said to Sue. "There's been an arrest for that Cranberry Lake murder."

Sue joined him in the den, sitting in the leather armchair with her long legs tucked beside her.

The arrest was the first item on the local news. The person charged with the murder of April Lovitt was twenty-year-old Jason Giddy. He and his girlfriend, a seventeen-year-old minor who could not be identified because of her age, had spent a day running up purchases on the victim's credit card. The young man denied killing April Lovitt. He had, he said, found the body in shallow water near the shore, taken the victim's backpack, and then shoved the body back into the water. The credit card had been in the backpack, which he later disposed of. Jason Giddy and his girlfriend both lived in the trailer park just outside Seeley's Bay. Giddy was known to the police.

On Monday morning Davey found a note in his pigeon-hole in the school office.

Two words: "Call me."

He knew what it must mean. At least Terry had the fore-sight to tell him first, before going to the police, so that he could be prepared. Fair warning. But he had to stop her. He went through the day like a robot, teaching mechanically, watching the clock.

At home, he roused himself. Sue had ordered a Christmas tree, which the man from the tree farm had delivered and set up in the living room. Sue had brought out the boxes of lights and decorations. *I may never have another chance to do this,* Davey thought as he stood on a chair to attach the star to the top of the tree. He might not have been a good husband, but he was a good father. Ten days to Christmas. Would this Christmas be his last as a family man?

While Sue read the girls a bedtime story, Davey poured two litres of milk down the kitchen sink. Then he went to the front hall and donned his overcoat, boots and hat. Sue, coming down the stairs, saw him pulling on his gloves.

"You aren't going out, are you? It's a terrible night."

"Just to the Hasti Mart. We're out of milk for breakfast."

"I don't think so. There were two unopened bags last time I looked. Let me check." She went into the kitchen.

In a moment she called, "I guess I was wrong, or else the girls got really thirsty."

"I'll be right back," Davey said.

With the freezing rain still falling, the street was like a skating rink. For traction he had to drive with the passenger-side wheels in the snowbanks that edged the curb. He parked around the corner from the hairdresser's salon, and walked there with his head bent, sleet lashing his cheeks.

Terry was startled when he let himself in.

"Why didn't you phone? You shouldn't go out on a night like this."

"You know I can't phone from home. And cellphone calls can be traced."

He took off his gloves, hat and coat, but not his boots.

"I thought I should tell you that I'm going to tell the police what I saw."

"For God's sake don't!"

"I have to. Giddy didn't kill that woman. He's innocent."

"Not that innocent. He has a record. B and E. Muggings. Corner-store holdups. Keep him locked up for twenty-five years and the world will be a safer place."

"You can't mean that."

"Terry, he's trailer park trash."

Her eyes were wide, watching him watching her.

"I was raised in a trailer park. And I'll tell you something else. Maybe you went to university and I didn't, but I know more about what's important than you do."

"Do you want to ruin my life?"

She laughed. "It looks like you wouldn't hesitate to ruin Jason Giddy's life, or mine, for that matter. So yes, it might give me a certain satisfaction."

Davey heard a groan and did not realize that it came from him. As he lunged, her hands flew up, and he saw the moonstone-and-silver bracelet on her slender wrist as he grabbed her neck. Her fingernails clawed at his hands. Her eyes bulged and reddened as his grip tightened. He heard the gurgle of air trapped in her closed-off throat.

In the end, it was silent and still. Terry lay crumpled on the floor, her long black hair spread like a fan. Sudden weakness came over him, and he sat down heavily on the sofa.

"Why did you make me do that?"

Davey looked at his hands as if he had never seen them before. When he finally managed to stop shaking, he put on his hat, his coat, and his gloves. Leaving Terry's apartment, he closed the door behind him. As he descended the steep staircase, he had to grip the banister to prevent himself from falling.

Ice coated the BMW. He had to scrape the windshield before he could drive away.

When he reached home, Sue met him in the hall.

"I've been worried. What took you so long?"

He looked at her, dazed, until he remembered his excuse for going out. "The Hasti Mart was closed, probably because of the ice storm. I drove around looking for someplace open." He pulled off his gloves. "It's murder out there."

"Did you get ..." Her voice faltered. "Did you get the milk?"

He shook his head. Words would not come. Sue unbuttoned his coat, helped him to doff it, then led him into the living room.

"You'd better tell me what happened."

The Christmas lights glowed, and the star shone from the top of the tree. When she pointed to the sofa, he sat down. She knelt facing him, her back to the Christmas tree. She was so close, kneeling between his thighs.

"Look at your hands."

"No." He turned his head aside. He could not bear to see the scratches oozing blood. Suddenly he was weeping.

"Davey. Tell me. What have you done?"

He choked on a sob. "I've killed a woman."

Sue stiffened. Her body pulled back, away from him. He heard the change in her breathing, how she fought to keep control. He felt his blood shiver colder and colder, and his mind cried out, *It is over, It is over.*

"Your mistress?"

"What!"

"Oh, I know all about her. Everybody knows. Terry Loucks. Isn't that ... wasn't that ... her name?" A pause. "What could she have done to you ... to deserve ... that?"

He buried his face in his hands, muffling his voice. "Remember the day you took the girls to Toronto to see *The Lion King?* I took Terry up to the cottage that afternoon. We saw Al Tofflemire with a girl in his canoe."

"Go on."

He looked up and saw that her eyes were on him. What did she see when she looked at him, what kind of monster? She did not interrupt.

When he had finished, she said, "So you were afraid that you would lose everything. Me. Kate and Sally. My money." He could see her throat working, trying to keep her voice steady.

"No," he sobbed. "It wasn't the money."

Her voice rose. "Don't lie. You've lied too much already. Those sordid little affairs with secretaries, filing clerks, classroom assistants!"

"You knew? Why did you stay?"

"Kate and Sally love you. You're a great father. When you're with the children, the best of you shines. Our daughters needed you in their lives every day, not just two weekends a month. Kicking you out would have devastated them. So I decided that I could bear the humiliation.

"Besides, I was sorry for you. I had money and you didn't. It was my money that took away your manhood. We didn't need your salary, and that bothered you. It hurts a man not to be necessary. That's why you turned to all those interchangeable women. They looked up to you."

"And you didn't."

"It hardly matters now." Sue rose. "That was a terrible thing you did. You must tell the police everything that you've told me."

"No!" He raised his face to her. "If I go to prison, think what that will do to Kate and Sally."

"To all of us."

"Then let's say nothing. Please, Sue, for the sake of the children. If the police ask questions, tell them I was here with you the entire evening."

She shook her head. "Look at your hands. Your skin tissue will be under her fingernails. Lies will not save you. I'll hire the best criminal lawyer in Canada and stand by you until the trial is over."

"And then what will you do, you and the children?"

"Leave the country, I suppose. Go back to using my maiden name."

Sue went into the hall and took the cordless phone from its cradle. Her hand was shaking as she brought it to him. "Phone 9-1-1. Ask for the police."

She faced him, dry-eyed. Behind her the tree lights shone.

"I'm sorry, Davey. You could have been a very good man."

Dead End

After three or four wrong turns, Margo Vandeep knew that she was lost.

Twenty minutes ago, she had driven through a crossroads where there was a general store, with a gas station kitty-corner from it. At the next spot she could turn around, she would try to retrace her route to find that crossroads again. Unless she found someone to give her directions, she would not get back to Flinton before dark.

After the crossroads there had been an abandoned railway station. No train tracks. Just the station standing alone in an empty field. It was a dilapidated wooden building with boarded-over windows and a weather-beaten sign announcing the name of the stop: Musgrove. Musgrove, she reasoned, must have been the name of the crossroads, back when it had a name.

She had stopped her car to take a picture of the abandoned railway station, for she was up here, north of Flinton, gathering material for the fourth book in her latest series, *Ontario's Lost Towns.*

Margo had already covered the Ottawa Valley, the Niagara Peninsula, and the north shore of Lake Erie. For this book she was researching the settlements of her own ancestors.

She knew little about her family's history. Whenever she had asked questions, Grandma Vandeep had advised, "Let sleeping dogs lie." Grandma had made only one visit "back home". That had been sixty years ago. She never talked about it.

Grandma's grandfather, Peter Vandeep (Margo's great-great-grandfather) had fled the region in 1870, at the age of twenty, leaving behind his parents, three sisters and seven brothers, none of whom he ever saw again.

"The Vandeeps were Late Loyalists," Grandma had told Margo, "too late to get any decent land. They found out that you couldn't push a plough through granite. Most gave up after two or three generations and moved south, like my grandfather. The rest turned to trapping and to guiding fishing parties in summer."

"Do I still have relatives living up there, north of Flinton?"

"You do," Grandma had replied. "But you don't want to know them."

When taking her photograph of the abandoned train station, Margo had wondered whether any of her forebears had ever stood at that spot, waiting for a train. Maybe it was from Musgrove that Peter Vandeep had started his journey south.

Margo's real name was Margery. It was her grandmother's name. As a child, she had considered it an okay name for an old lady. But girls called Margery were plain and wore ugly clothes. Twenty years ago, when she was a senior ready to graduate from her Toronto high school, she had seen the need to reinvent herself. Starting university, she introduced herself as Margo, and never thought of herself as a Margery again.

To cast aside the name was easy. But there was no way she could have altered the physical features that had been passed down to her. Pale blue eyes. A long, cleft chin.

With a different chin – smaller and softer – she would have been a pretty woman. Not that she was ugly. People used words like "striking" to describe her. Men found her attractive. Ten years ago a civil engineer named Harry Bowman had wanted to marry her. If she had accepted, he would have carried her off to distant lands to live the empty life of an ex-pat wife. Margo had escaped in the nick of time.

As her career advanced, her work came to absorb her totally. Her illustrated guidebook, *London: City with a Past,* had sold out three printings and been reissued in a new edition. On the whole she was satisfied with her life.

Margo prided herself on her sense of direction. She had never been lost before. Other people might need those GPS devices, but not her. Yet here she was, in the middle of nowhere, with a useless map that did not mark the remote concessions north of Flinton, few of which had signs.

On her left rose a granite cliff; on her right was a bog. No room to make a U-turn. No lanes where she could turn around. She had driven two kilometres without seeing a hydro line or a telephone pole, and certainly no sign of a house or a barn.

She was beginning to suspect that the region was uninhabited when unexpectedly, at the end of a barely-perceptible lane, she saw a house. At the point where the lane began, the road came to a dead end.

It was a frame house, two storeys high. If there hadn't been smoke rising from the chimney, she would have taken for granted that the place was deserted. In the weeds beside the house sat an old car with spoke wheels and no tires on the rims.

Margo nosed her car into the lane, which consisted of two ruts with tall weeds growing between them. If she had been driving an ATV and not a Nissan hatchback, she might have driven right up to the house. But maybe not. She wasn't certain she wanted to knock on the door. Who knew what sort of person would answer?

She stopped the car and glanced at the fuel gauge. Less than a quarter of a tank. Reluctantly she turned off the ignition. If she hadn't been low on gas, she would have left the engine running.

As she stepped out of the car, she saw a downstairs window curtain twitch. How often, she wondered, did an automobile come up this road?

She walked up to the house and stepped onto the rickety board that rested on two concrete blocks in front of the door. Before she had a chance to knock, the door opened.

In front of Margo stood a woman who was ninety years old if she was a day. She had skimpy white hair hanging loose, watery blue eyes, sunken cheeks, and a long cleft chin. Her faded dress sagged from her narrow shoulders. Like the house, the dress seemed to be no colour at all.

The old woman peered at her.

"Good evening," Margo said. "I wonder if you could give me directions back to Flinton. You see –"

At the sound of Margo's voice, the woman's wrinkled face cracked into a smile, revealing yellowed teeth and a gap where one upper incisor was missing.

"Well, if it ain't Margery!"

Margo nearly tumbled from the board.

"I'm sorry, but you mistake me for someone else. You've never seen me before."

The woman ignored Margo's explanation. Perhaps she was deaf.

"Daddy and me bin countin' every day for sixty years, waitin' for you to come back like you promised you would."

Before Margo knew what was happening, she found herself pulled inside. The old woman's crooked fingers were like talons gripping her arm.

"I've never been here before!" Margo protested, trying to pull free.

"Don't tell me that! You're Margery Vandeep, or else I'm the Pope of Rome. Oh, you look different since you visited us before, but there's no mistakin' those blue eyes and that chin. You're a Vandeep all right."

"Vandeep?" Margo shuddered. At that instant, she felt cold as ice. "Are you … a Vandeep?"

"Have I changed so much you don't know me? I'm your aunt Emmeline – well, really, it's first cousin once removed. But I told you to call me Aunt Emmeline because I'm fifteen years older than you. Now you just set down and I'll fix some supper. The spare bedroom's waitin' for you. After all, you did promise to come back."

The woman did not loosen her grip until Margo sat down on a wooden chair. Should I make a run for it? she wondered. Probably, yes. But curiosity grabbed her as tightly as the old woman's fingers had done. Should it become necessary, she could easily escape.

Aunt Emmeline tottered across the room to an enamel sink set in a wooden counter. In one corner of the counter sat a baited mousetrap. Above the counter, a dozen tins of Heinz pork and beans stood on a wooden shelf. She lifted one tin from the shelf and began to saw off the lid with a straight, old-fashioned can opener.

"Daddy's goin' to be so happy to see you."

Daddy? Margo thought. Nobody her age has their father still alive.

"He took to bed right after you left. Since that day, he's spent all his time sleepin'. He's an old man, my husband."

"I thought you called him Daddy."

"Well, so I did."

"Let me get this straight. Are you a Vandeep by birth or by marriage?"

"Both, as you very well know. My father was a Vandeep, and I married one."

Margo was tempted to quip, Not the same one, I hope? But who knew what the answer might be? She changed the subject.

"I need to get back to Flinton before dark. I'm afraid I took a couple of wrong turns. If you could just tell me the way …"

"You'd never make if before dark. You'd end up stuck in the bog, drowned in Buck Lake, or else wrapped around a tree. But you ain't goin' to Flinton anyway. This is the place where you belong."

Aunt Emmeline stooped to lift a split log from a wooden crate that stood beside a Quebec heater in one corner of the room. Using a wad of rags as a protective mitt, she opened the door of the heater and eased the log inside. She turned to Margo. "Watch the stairs when you go up to your room. Second step from the top got a broken tread. Your cousin Kyle broke his neck when he tripped on that one and fell down the stairs. Kyle's room is right next to yours." She paused. "And another thing, don't mind any noises you hear in the night. This is an old house. The walls are filled with voices."

"Really, I must go." Margo stood up.

"Now Margery, you ain't goin' to leave us again. Daddy would be so disappointed. Before I put this on the stove, I'll just tell him you're here." She crossed the floor to a door at the back of the room and grasped the china doorknob.

When Aunt Emmeline opened the door, Margo saw that the room held a double bed with a woman's grey flannel nightgown lying across the foot. Someone appeared to be in the bed, under a patchwork quilt. Someone? Something?

On one of the pillows lay a mummified head, a human skull covered with brown parchment skin. The nose was fallen in, the eyes sealed. Strands of white hair clung to the scalp.

Aunt Emmeline approached the bed. "Daddy!" She leaned over the pillow on which the mummified head rested. "Wake up! Margery's come back!"

Margo bolted.

As she leapt over the sill, she heard Aunt Emmeline shriek, "Don't you be leavin' us now!"

Margo was halfway to the car before Aunt Emmeline, leaning on her cane, had stepped down from the rickety board to hobble in pursuit.

Her cracked voice followed Margo. "Margery! Margery!"

Margo locked the car door. Without fastening her seatbelt, she turned the ignition key and held her breath until the engine started. She backed onto the road. Then she was off, rear wheels spinning in the gravel.

On her left, heavy mist smothered the bog. If she had slowed down one second earlier, she might have avoided the spot where the road shoulder had crumbled away. Too late, she jammed on the brakes, clutching the steering wheel as the left front wheel skidded over. The car tipped and then, as if in slow motion, nosed over the bank. She jolted forwards, unrestrained, and heard a thump as her head hit the glass. For a few minutes she sat stunned, her hand pressed to her forehead. Then she turned off the ignition.

Through the mist and twilight haze she saw that the Nissan's grille was deep in muck. Tall rushes surrounded the hood, but the driver's door was not blocked. Only a few metres of mud and swamp water stood between her and firm earth, but a tow truck would be needed to pull her car back onto the road.

The window on the driver side was partly open, admitting the fetid smell of decaying vegetation. The shrill hum of mosquitoes cut through the booming, croaking and peeping of innumerable frogs. She felt a mosquito bite behind her ear. Margo swatted it and then closed the window.

No need to panic. She had her cellphone. If she called 9-1-1, the police could track her position. They would contact the Canadian Automobile Association to send a tow truck to pull her out of this bog.

Opening her cell, she pressed the button. With a chime, the screen lit up: "Searching for Network." And then: "No Service." Up here in the Canadian Shield, that was no surprise.

Returning the phone to her handbag, she considered what to do. The crossroads lay somewhere ahead. Maybe five kilometres. Maybe ten. In the morning she would set out on foot to find it. The gas station would have a tow truck. But for now, she was stuck.

Margo raised her hand to her throbbing forehead. There would be a big goose egg, but no serious harm. The windshield glass wasn't even cracked.

She might as well settle down. There was little chance of another car coming along this road before morning, and that was just as well. Although Good Samaritans do show up from time to time, the innocent traveller is just as likely to fall among thieves.

This backcountry was likely crawling with Vandeeps. The three sisters and seven brothers that Peter Vandeep had left behind in 1870 had had one hundred and forty years to propagate. And what else, she thought wryly, was there to do in the country north of Flinton?

Grandma, who had made her one visit "back home" sixty years ago, must be the Margery whom Aunt Emmeline remembered. Next time Margo saw her grandmother, she would ask about Aunt Emmeline, Daddy and Cousin Kyle. She would pry from her the truth about that visit.

Senility could explain why Aunt Emmeline mistook Margo for the cousin who had visited sixty years ago. But dementia could not explain keeping a corpse in her bed for six decades.

"He took to bed right after you left. Since that day, he spends all his time sleepin'."

For Margo, as for her grandmother, one visit "back home" would be more than enough. She already had sufficient material for her book. Twenty-four hours from now, she would be back in Toronto, in her comfortable apartment, sipping Campari and soda. But right now she had eight hours to kill. She might as well use the time to write up notes on the photographs taken today.

Or she could draft a letter. There was one that she needed to write, a letter to the man who had been her lover ten years ago. Harry Bowman. After being out of the country for years, he had contacted her recently on his return. Tentatively, shyly, they had met for dinner.

It would amuse Harry, she thought, to receive a letter written at night in a bog. Or should she confess her predicament? She would hate to sound like the kind of helpless woman who needs a man to save her. Actually, Harry would like that. He would enjoy nothing more than an opportunity to rescue her from a bog ... a raging bull ... or any kind of danger. That's the sort of man he was.

Harry was a builder of roads, bridges and tunnels, a project manager who lived for years at a stretch in countries like Peru and Bulgaria. After she turned him down, he had married someone else. It had not worked out. Harry was single again.

He had found her again at a time when she was ready to rethink what she was doing with her life. Harry was a good man, attractive and interesting. Thirty-seven was not too old for a woman to bear children. Now she could see herself as part of a family. A fruitful family. And there would be no need to give up her career. Living in foreign lands, she could write a new series of travel books, photograph ruins of ancient civilizations.

A warm feeling spread through her. Margo opened a new file and began to write.

"Hello Harry," was as far as she got before she heard a bump on the window right at her ear.

Margo jumped. Turning her head, she saw outside the glass a big hairy moth that had been attracted by the light from her monitor. With a laugh, she settled down to write more.

"Sorry not to have written sooner, but I have been busy driving around the back roads north of Flinton, which is a place you've probably never heard of. Some of the roads are little more than cow paths, and none are marked."

She paused, her hands over the keyboard. Should she tell him that she was writing this letter while stuck in a bog? Yes, she decided. Let him see that she could make fun of herself.

"As a matter of fact, I am sitting in my car stuck in a bog as I …"

Margo heard another bump against the window glass. A tapping sound. She turned her head, expecting another moth.

A big man with scraggly hair and a long, cleft chin peered at her through the glass.

"Need some help?"

She shook her head rapidly from side to side.

"Open the door!"

When she did not, he lifted a tire iron with both hands and aimed it at the door handle.

Hilda Perly

"Are you packed?"

From the hall, Fyler saw Hildy's suitcase sitting open and empty on the carpet just inside the bedroom door. With the drapes pulled, the room was dark. Hildy lay on her back under an afghan on their king-size bed. Her eyes were shut. She was clutching an ice pack to her forehead.

"What?" she moaned.

"I said, 'Are you packed?'"

"No. I'm not."

"Well, you'd better get started." He switched on the overhead light.

"My God, Fyler! Are you trying to kill me?"

"Snap out of it." Hildy always managed to work up a migraine when there was something she didn't want to do. "Unless we leave within half an hour, we're going to miss our flight."

"For God's sake, go by yourself and give me a break."

"Don't be ridiculous."

He left the door ajar when he returned to the living room. From there he could hear any sounds of packing, except there were none to hear. He stood beside the piano, lighting a cigarette.

The piano was a Steinway grand. A grouping of photographs in silver frames stood on it: their daughter Carla at her university graduation, smiling; their son Earl at his Call to the Bar, smiling; and in the third photograph, Hildy standing next to an even grander grand piano with her accompanist, Geraldo Rossi, slightly out of focus in the background. Hildy, too, was smiling. At Hildy's throat was the diamond necklace Fyler had given her in honour of her farewell concert. Her final aria had been *Vissi d'arte, vissi d'amore.* ("Love and music, these have I lived for").

"The demands of a career in music require too many sacrifices on the part of my family," she had explained at her final press conference.

It had been her decision. He had not asked her to abandon her career. She could have gone on. To the Met. To La Scala. It was all within her reach. She was good enough. He wouldn't have held her back.

When she told him that she was going to retire, he had asked her, "Are you sure?" He had even tried – admittedly, not too hard – to talk her out of it.

He looked again at the photograph, remembering the glow on Hildy's face as she bowed and bowed, her arms loaded with roses, before leaving the stage for the last time.

After her retirement she would neither perform nor practise. From that night on, her glorious voice sang only lullabies. Perfect mother. But defensive. She seemed to glory in having given up so much. Martyrdom, he came to suspect, was her new career.

Some people still remembered her. Only a few months ago, a woman at a cocktail party had asked, "Didn't you used to be Hilda Perly?"

"That was before I became Hildy Gant," she had laughed. "A different life."

"Once, in Los Angles, I heard you sing."

"I haven't done that for a long, long time."

Twenty-five years, in fact.

Fifteen minutes passed. Still no sounds of packing. Fyler strode into the bedroom.

"Come on! It's time to go."

"I'm not ready. I have nothing packed."

"I'll buy you a toothbrush at the airport."

Hildy sat up, swung her legs over the side of the bed, and leaned forward, her long blond hair hanging over her face.

"I can't go to Calgary carrying an empty suitcase."

"Fine. I'll fill it for you." Fyler pulled open her closet door, yanked armfuls of jackets and blouses from their hangers, and dumped them into the suitcase. "There! Now you've got something to carry." When he had done up the suitcase's zipper and straps, he checked his watch. "Put your shoes on. We're leaving."

Alarm set. Door locked. If the traffic was not too bad, they could still make their flight.

He glanced at Hildy, slumped in the Porsche's passenger seat. These headaches had been going on for months. It was no picnic to be married to a woman who developed a migraine every time he expected anything from her. And he expected so little! All she had to do was look good and make pleasant conversation four or five times a year.

Bumper to bumper all the way to the 401. Everybody was heading out of Toronto for the Victoria Day weekend. He drummed his fingers on the steering wheel.

Damn Hildy! Considering all he had to put up with, wasn't it ironic that he alone, of all the partners in Switt, Gant, Sanders, and McGill, had never been divorced? His colleagues envied him. At least Joe Sanders did.

Just last month Joe had come into his office late at night. Fyler was still there, working on a file.

After a few pleasantries, Joe had commented, "You're lucky you found someone like Hildy first time around."

"Yeah, I've been lucky." Fyler had shuffled a few papers, to show that he needed to get back to work.

But Joe had planted himself in the doorway. "I've struck out three times. Now I pay twenty thousand a month in child support. Each of my ex-wives lives in a house I paid for. Fyler, you just see me driving around in my silver Mercedes. Would you believe it? After thirty years practising corporate law, that car is the only thing I own."

Fyler had answered. "I don't know how you guys can live, supporting two or three households."

"Live? I wouldn't call it that."

Joe returned to his office. He worked late every night.

To all appearances – and appearances counted for a lot – Hildy was perfect. Companion, travel partner, and mother to his children. And she looked good – at least, she had looked good until the headaches started. A couple every week. Change of life? Did menopausal women always get weird?

There were two Hildys now. So far, the right one had always shown up when it mattered. But it was a strain never to know how she would be from one day to the next. Sometimes he wondered how his life would be without Hildy. In many respects, he liked the idea.

"I'm going to be sick."

Her whimper brought him back to reality.

"Try not to get it on the upholstery."

She leaned forward, still wearing her seatbelt, and threw up on the floor mat.

Fyler's stomach gave a lurch.

They made it to the airport. As soon as Fyler and Hildy had settled in their first-class seats, she appeared to feel better. By the time the plane had burst through the clouds, her colour was coming back.

Luckily, her clothes had escaped the deluge. Crossing his fingers, Fyler hoped she could manage four days without a migraine. As soon as they were back in Toronto, he would insist that she see a doctor. Enough was enough.

Reaching their hotel, they had an hour free before the opening reception. Their room on the twenty-second floor was waiting for them. With the makeup she carried in her handbag, Hildy touched up her lips and eyes. Then she arranged her hair in a French twist. The grab bag of clothes that Fyler had dumped into her suitcase happened to include two items – only two – that went together: a little black jacket with lacy sleeves over a smoky grey camisole.

"You look elegant," he told her when she had finished.

She smiled.

At the reception, Fyler worked the room, keeping an eye on Hildy. She seemed happy, greeting acquaintances with hugs and air kisses. He lost track of her for half an hour, and then spotted her seated on a sofa, deep in conversation with an elderly gentleman. The man had white hair that brushed his collar, and a long nose. Hildy was leaning toward him, as if intent upon hearing his every word above the buzz and chatter in the room.

The elderly gentleman wore black tie. Absurdly overdressed, Fyler thought. But after a moment he realized that the man was not a lawyer but merely one of the musicians who were to play for them later. He and Hildy must be talking about music for the conversation to have brought such animation to her face.

Fyler picked up another glass of wine and joined a group of lawyers who were discussing the litigation that resulted from the oil spill of the *Exxon Valdez* back in 1989. He wanted a cigarette, and after a few minutes broke away from the group to walk out onto the wide, open deck where smoking was allowed. It was nine o'clock, and dusk was falling. As he stood by the railing, the street lights came on. In the garden below, the yellow flowers of the forsythia shimmered like gold dust along the brick pathways.

When he went back inside, a string quartet was playing something baroque. And there was Hildy's new friend, a cello between his legs and his bow tenderly stroking the strings. He was not as elderly as Fyler had thought. Hildy stood at the edge of the small group that was actually paying attention to the music, her expression rapt.

Fyler picked up another glass of wine, satisfied. He had been right to bring her to Calgary.

When he rejoined the group that had been talking about the *Exxon Valdez,* the discussion had moved on to legal fees, with varied opinions on appropriate tariffs for the lawyers in class action suits.

Twenty minutes later, the musical interlude at an end, Fyler saw that Hildy had resumed her seat on the sofa. She was again conversing with the not-so-elderly cellist.

At Fyler's approach, both stood. She introduced the cellist as Viktor Vaghy. Fyler said that he had enjoyed the music but now it was getting late.

"Thank you, Hilda," Mr. Vaghy said in a faint Hungarian accent. "We shall continue this tomorrow."

"I'll look forward to that."

He took her hand and raised it to his lips.

"Continue what?" Fyler asked.

"We were discussing *Fidelio,*" she said, slowly withdrawing her hand from Mr. Vaghy's.

"*Fidelio?* That's Beethoven's opera, isn't it? I've never actually heard it."

"I sang Leonore once," Hildy said. "Before I met you."

Fyler took Hilda's hand in such a way that Mr. Vaghy could not fail to notice. Leading her away, he observed, "He called you *Hilda*."

"Yes. He recognized me. When he called me Hilda, I saw no reason to correct him."

Fyler steered her toward the elevators. "It's time we both got some rest. And you've had a rough day." He pushed the 'up' button on the panel.

"Fyler, I'm fine now. Tomorrow I need to buy clothes. I asked at the desk. The best shop is called *La Chic.* I can take a cab there."

"I don't think you ought to see that Vaghy fellow tomorrow. There's something about him I don't like. Why don't you go to the Glenbow Museum after you've done shopping? That's what I'd do, if I had time."

"But you never have time, do you?"

He noticed the criticism. "I'm here to work. Tomorrow I have an all-day session on tax evasion."

She laughed. "How to do it?"

She was merry, all of a sudden.

"No," he said severely. "It helps the defendant's solicitor to know what the Canada Revenue Agency thinks his client may have done."

His tone sobered her. They rode in silence to the twenty-second floor.

Their room was spacious, with two double beds. As he undressed, he caught Hildy watching him, her brow furrowed, looking as if there were something she wanted to say. Whatever it was, he did not want to hear it. That Vaghy fellow had unsettled him, calling her Hilda like that. Why shouldn't he feel threatened? At fifty-two, Hildy was an attractive woman, with a figure that looked ten years younger. When he looked at her in the right light – providing she didn't have a migraine – he could still see the glamorous diva whose voice had soared at Massey Hall the first time he heard her.

He had gone on a free ticket with one of the partners, Alistair McGill, a subscriber whose wife for some reason had been unable to attend. Afterwards, there had been a reception in the private lounge for the concert series' patrons and benefactors.

"Do you want to meet Hilda Perly?" Alistair had asked. "Some of these musicians are interesting people."

"Yes. I'd like to meet her. She's gorgeous. And what a voice!"

Smitten even before he met her, Fyler made his move as fast as he could. To attract her attention had not been easy. Chocolates were a cliché. Too many people sent flowers for that to make an impression. But he was an up-and-coming lawyer. Early-thirties. Well-dressed. Money to spend. He thought she might be tired of touring, of staying in a different hotel in a different city every night. It turned out that he was right. She cut down the touring after they married, and reduced her schedule even more when Earl was born. Then she gave it up for good. He was happy. He had assumed that she was, too.

Hildy was still sleeping when he left their hotel room in the morning.

When he returned in the middle of the afternoon, he found her stretched out on her bed. *Oh, no! Not another migraine!* But her eyes were open, and when she saw his anxious look, she smiled.

Then he noticed the pink, rectangular box lying on the easy chair by the window. It was labelled, *"La Chic"*.

"Did you buy something nice?"

"Nice? I bought a skirt you might call nice. But the gown I'll be wearing Saturday evening to the formal dinner is anything but."

Fyler looked at her askance. He had not thought about the convention's closing banquet; of course she would need a gown. What did she mean by, "anything but ..."?

"Want to see it? I'll model it for you." She rose from the bed, picked up the box, and opened the bathroom door. "This will take a few minutes."

Fyler removed his shoes and lay down. Outside the big plate-glass window, the sky was translucent blue. He watched a hawk circling, and he wished that he could have a cigarette. Unfortunately, this was a non-smoking room.

Hildy emerged.

The gown was blue, the same cornflower blue as her eyes. It was strapless, sparkling with sequins, and cut so low her breasts looked ready to pop out over the top. The skirt was long and tight, with a side slit halfway up her shapely thigh.

He gasped. "Hildy! You can't wear that to a Law Society dinner. What were you thinking?" He looked at his watch. "It's just four o'clock. I can go with you right now to take it back. We'll find something more appropriate."

And then the oddest thing happened.

Hildy said no. It was not a passive no, the kind he could circumvent by waiting. She looked combative. Her eyes narrowed. Her jaw jutted.

"I'm keeping this dress."

"It's not suitable."

"You saw what Sophie Milman wore last December when she sang at Massey Hall."

"Sophie Milman is half your age. And a Law Society dinner isn't Massey Hall."

Hildy cocked her head in a defiant way.

"I intend to wear it for my European tour."

"Your what?"

Suddenly Fyler felt like a man in a foreign country, dropped into the Arrivals area where everyone around him spoke a language he did not understand.

"I had lunch with Viktor. We talked about music. About what I'd done. The kind of things I still might do. He says that in Europe the mature woman has more value. She is still desired."

He heard Hildy's words, but their implication was so improbable that he could not believe what his ears told him.

He breathed slowly. "When we get back to Toronto, you need to see a doctor."

"Why? Do you think I'm nuts? Kiri Te Kanawa was at the peak of her career when she was my age."

"You haven't sung for twenty-five years."

He had a memory of *Sunset Boulevard*, and horror swept over him that Hildy was about to make a fool of herself, and of him as well.

"It's still here. My voice. I feel it inside me." And she touched her fingers to her throat.

He grabbed her wrist, holding it so tight that tears sprang to her eyes. She tried to pull away.

"Let me go! That hurts!"

"I want to hear you sing. Then I'll let you go."

He heard her suck in wind – *wihhh* –

"Sing!"

She shook her head, confused, and he realized that she did not know what to sing, or how to go about it at all. Then her mouth opened.

"Un bel di, vedremo, levarsi un fil di fumo …" ("One fine day, we'll see a thread of smoke arising …")

It was a high, reedy voice that cracked from fear. He released her wrist. The song stopped.

It was as if a plug had been pulled, the juice cut off. The room was utterly still. She stared at him, wide-eyed. His arms hung at his sides and he wondered whether to put them around her, but he just stood there, afraid to breathe.

"That wasn't fair," she said, "but you've made your point." She turned her back, and Fyler understood it was because she was crying. "I need to be alone." Her voice trembled. "Give me twenty minutes to change. Then we'll take the gown back to *La Chic*."

"Are you sure you're all right?"

"Yes. I'm fine. Not to worry. Please."

He went down to the bar and ordered a double Scotch. It was gone in two gulps. His hands shook. He had another double. It did not stop the shaking of his hands. Then he returned to the room.

Hildy was gone. So were the blue gown and her suitcase. The rectangular box lay open and empty, its tissue paper tossed onto the floor.

Shuddering, he went out onto the balcony, half expecting to see her body and a sprung-open suitcase, a blue gown, and a scattering of other garments on the pavement twenty-two storeys below. But everything looked normal. The flow of traffic and the march of pedestrians went on, in choreographed obedience to the changing of the lights.

"Thank God!" he exclaimed.

He went back inside and sat on his bed, waiting for her return. Hildy had these crazy moments, but she always came through when it mattered. He watched a movie without having any idea what it was about. When it was time for dinner, he showered, put on a fresh shirt, and went down alone.

He told the others at his table that his wife had been forced to leave suddenly, that she had gone back to Ontario on receiving news that her mother was ill. This story would serve as well as another to explain her absence for the rest of the conference.

Now, with utter clarity of vision, he foresaw that Hildy would not be back. He did not feel angry. There was something life-affirming in her departure. He felt a kind of pride in her. In both of them, really, because no one who knew them could have seen it coming. As long as their marriage had lasted, not a crack had shown. Now all that remained was to tidy things up with a minimum of fuss.

One year after the final decree, Fyler was sitting at his desk, working on a file, when Joe Sanders appeared at his open door.

"Are you busy?" Joe asked. "There's something I want to tell you."

"Go ahead. This isn't urgent." Fyler looked up from his computer screen.

"I'm going to …" Joe flushed. "I'm going to give it one more try."

"You're getting married?" Fyler shook his head, and then he laughed and rose to his feet. "Let's go for a drink. To celebrate your courage."

"You think I'm crazy?"

"Maybe not crazy, but certainly a slow learner. What's that line? 'Hope springs eternal in the human breast.'"

It was close to Christmas, and cold outside. As they hurried up the street, they passed a fashion window with mannequins in evening gowns, a glittering silver Christmas tree, and a pyramid of silver boxes with gold bows. The display made him think of Hildy and the blue gown from *La Chic*.

Joe and Fyler ducked into the first pub they came to. Both ordered single malt. Joe asked about Hildy.

"She's living in Budapest," Fyler said.

"You in touch?"

"Not me. Our daughter Carla went over to see her. Hildy's living with a cellist, and she's learning to speak Magyar." He paused. "She calls herself Hilda Perly. She sings in a cabaret."

Devil's Eye

"Ida, today you can take me to Goodwill," my mother said when I picked her up at the Golden Years Retirement Village. "I need a new raincoat."

Ninety per cent of our weekly excursions brought us to Goodwill, where I would follow her up and down the aisles between displays of gently-used merchandise, Mom in her slow progress leaning on the hickory cane that had been her father's, and his father's before that. My mother had been reusing and recycling since long before my generation noticed a need to save the planet. A child of the Dirty Thirties, she was programmed from birth to save string.

I pulled up in the Goodwill parking lot. After a week of April showers, it was dotted with shimmering, grease-coated puddles.

"I wonder if they'll have a Burberry or a London Fog," she said as we navigated around the water-filled potholes, my hand under her elbow. "I want a raincoat that will last as long as I do."

Today she was in luck. One Burberry and two London Fogs were hanging on the same rack. I left her to deliberate and wandered off – but not far – in search of diversion.

On a table stocked with handbags, a Gucci caught my eye. It was black, in an elegant textured fabric, with a clasp shaped like a buckle, bright as chrome. The leather binding was a little worn. Still, a thousand-dollar handbag for five bucks! We women are our mothers' daughters. I picked it up. Rarely do I purchase anything at Goodwill, but something told me that I must buy this bag.

After stopping at the Golden Years Retirement Village to drop off my mother and her new-to-her London Fog, I drove home.

Mitch was in the living room, sunk into his favourite armchair, reading the current issue of the *Journal of Applied Psychology.* His tie was loosened and the top button of his shirt undone. He had tossed his suit jacket over the footstool. Mitch always wore a suit, unlike faculty in the Humanities, who dressed so casually I could barely tell them from the students.

"Where did you get that?" he asked, as I set the Gucci bag on the coffee table.

"At Goodwill."

"It looks expensive."

"Five dollars," I said proudly.

"Did you need a new purse?"

Having made his point, Mitch returned to his reading.

My husband, Dr. Mitchell Blackburn, taught Organizational Behaviour in the School of Business at Melrose University. An expert on personality testing, he subscribed

163

to dozens of scholarly journals and read them constantly. This was necessary, he had explained to me, in order to keep up with the theories of rival gurus, which he exploded regularly in articles of his own.

I seated myself on the sofa. Picking up the Gucci, I peered inside. It was not one of those organizer handbags for the woman who needs "a place for everything and everything in its place". The Gucci was more like an empty sack, with only one separate zippered compartment. I opened this compartment now, hoping, like any woman who ever bought a second-hand purse, to find money inside. What I found was a marble.

I pulled it out. It was a large marble – nearly one inch in diameter – blood-red glass with a yellow wedge in the centre.

"Look!" I held it up between thumb and forefinger. "A marble." Mitch pursed his lips and frowned while his eyes remained on the page. "Mitch, have you ever seen one like this?"

Now he did look up.

"That's a boulder." His eyebrows lifted. "Let me see." I handed it to him. He examined it for a moment. "Devil's Eye. I collected marbles when I was a kid, but I never got my hands on one of these."

"Maybe it's valuable."

"Could be. I have a colleague, Bill Lipinsky, who collects marbles. He's an expert." Mitch gave the marble back to me. "I'll ask Bill about it. It might be worth something." Mitch returned to his journal.

Now I looked more closely at the marble. Held up against the light, the blood-red glass appeared to liquefy and the yellow wedge to swell. I shivered. No wonder they called it a Devil's Eye.

With the Gucci bag over my arm and the marble cradled in the palm of my hand, I left Mitch to his journal and went upstairs. My intention was to put the handbag on my closet shelf. As for the marble, it could go back where I had found it. I couldn't think of any better place to keep it safe until I knew whether it was valuable or not.

No sooner had I dropped the marble into the Gucci's inner compartment, than a voice cried: "Let me out of here!"

The voice came from the handbag. It was masculine and humanoid. A bit like Mitch's voice.

"Pardon me?" I hesitated. Purses do not talk.

"I've been trapped in here for ten years."

Apparently it was the marble, not the handbag, speaking. I did not answer. This was one of Mitch's tricks. He was an old hand at devising tests to measure my emotional intelligence. The closet was probably bugged. If I were a clever woman – which I am not – I might have been more appreciative of his efforts to identify areas of my personality needing development. Being married to Mitch was sometimes overwhelming. I needed time to think.

"I'm not going to talk to you," I said. "You are a marble. We are not on speaking terms." But out of compassion I lifted it from the handbag. The marble was hot in my hand.

Its yellow eye pulsed as it spoke again: "Take Golden Boy, 150 to one."

I blinked. Who was Golden Boy? And where was I supposed to take him?

"I have to cook dinner." I set the marble on the dainty porcelain plate on my dressing table, next to a safety pin. Okay, I've lost my mind, I thought. I must never breathe a word of this to Mitch. I turned my back on the marble.

"Watch NASDAQ!" it called as I left the bedroom. "Tech stocks soar!"

When Mitch met me back in the nineteen seventies, I was one of the girls in the typing pool in the School of Business office, leading an uncomplicated life. Working on his first book in the days before Microsoft invented *Word,* Mitch was aware that his otherwise impressive skill set did not include typing or spelling. And so he hired me to spend ten hours a week, evenings and weekends, working with him to prepare his manuscript for submission. Mitch was a brilliant man. We both thought that he was God.

We worked at his apartment, since all his files were there. This arrangement made me the envy of all the girls in the office. Mitch was the only eligible bachelor in the School of Business. I can't say that he paid me well, but my status in the typing pool went way up. At coffee breaks every day the other girls questioned me about Mitch.

I didn't tell them the really interesting stuff. I mean, if you put a normal man and an eager-to-please girl together in an apartment for ten hours a week, sex is bound to happen. Mitch was attractive in a rumpled kind of way, for it was only after his second book that he discovered suits and shoe polish. I was slender in those days, with almond-shaped grey eyes and ash blond hair. Still, when the book was finished and our arrangement came to an end, I was almost as surprised as the girls in the office when Mitch asked me to marry him.

Looking back on it, I think he regarded me much as Professor Higgins regarded Eliza Doolittle. I was a project – raw material he could fashion into a perfect faculty wife.

When he married me, I was "woefully undereducated", as he frequently pointed out not only to me but also to anyone who cared to listen. He picked out the books I needed to read, but I don't think I got all the way through a single one of them.

Thinking about my talking marble, I was quiet at dinner. Mitch did not notice. If anything, he was grateful for silence. He was working with a postgrad student, concocting tests that businesses could use to detect hidden personality traits in prospective employees. The student's name was Elena. Mitch was having an affair with her. I didn't mind; it got him out of the house.

As soon as we had finished eating, he left for his lab. I loaded the dishwasher, and then went upstairs to the bedroom. The marble, sitting on its porcelain plate, was watching me. Its yellow eye pulsed at my approach.

"08-10-14-24-27-28. Lotto 649."

I looked into the marble's yellow, pulsing eye. "That's a lottery number!"

"08-10-14-24-27-28. Lotto 649."

"Mitch calls lotteries a tax on the poor. He says only fools play the lottery."

"08-10-14-24-27-28. Lotto 649." The marble had a deep, commanding voice, and as it spoke, its centre throbbed like a beating heart.

The marble was insistent. It repeated the number again. I grabbed a pencil and wrote it down. Why not? I asked myself. Mitch will never know.

It was a pleasant spring evening. I put on my coat and strolled to the Hasti Mart three blocks from our house and bought a ticket.

After returning home, I put the ticket for safekeeping in the same compartment of the purse where the marble had been. It was now eleven o'clock, and Mitch was still out. As I undressed, my eyes kept turning to the marble, which lay still and silent on the porcelain plate.

"You won't tell Mitch, will you?" I said to the marble. "Promise you won't!"

Not a peep came from it. The pulsing had stopped. It was hard to believe that this insignificant bit of glass had spoken, and so forcibly! Maybe I had imagined the whole incident. Possibly I was going insane. Thirty-five years of living with Mitch could do that. All that testing had warped my brain.

According to Mitch, I'd never had much of a brain to begin with. But I was a fair cook and an okay housekeeper. I suppose I was an adequate mother, since both our kids turned out all right. But that could have been despite my mothering, rather than because of it.

Whenever I did or said something particularly hopeless, Mitch would sit me down and, resting his elbows on the arms of his chair, place his hands together so that his fingers made five little steeples. "Ida," he would say, letting out an exasperated sigh, "I wish you would help solve your intellectual issues instead of fighting against them."

At one point, about twenty years ago, I had expected him to dump me in favour of a grad student assistant named Kimberley. I quivered every time he said, "Ida, we must talk."

Now it's coming, I would think. But no. After Kimberley, there was Susanna, and then Mary Beth. The grad students came and went. I stayed.

I didn't understand why he put up with me until I heard him comment on the divorce of one of his colleagues. Mitch said, "I can't believe that a man who teaches business could get himself into a situation where he has to split his assets."

Days went by. The marble stayed put, lying on my dressing table. Since the first day, it had not uttered a word.

"You're just a piece of glass," I said to it one morning while making the bed. "You can't talk. You never could talk. Stupid marble! How dare you make me feel like an idiot!"

"Who are you talking to?"

I jumped. For an instant I thought it was the marble speaking.

"Oh, Mitch! I thought you'd gone to work."

"Left my car keys somewhere. Came back to look for them." He spotted them on top of the chest of drawers. "Ah! Here they are."

He was putting the keys into his pocket when he spied the marble on its dainty plate. "Hey! I told Bill Lipinsky about your marble." Mitch picked it up. "He says if it's a genuine Devil's Eye in mint condition, he'll give two hundred for it."

"Wow!" I said, just like one of those people on the *Antiques Roadshow* when they're told that grandpa's chamber pot is worth a million dollars.

When Mitch left, taking the marble with him, sadness came over me. I was sorry that I'd spoken roughly to it. Soon I was crying like a baby, sitting on the edge of the half-made bed with tears trickling down my cheeks. I half hoped that Bill Lipinsky would reject my Devil's Eye as imperfect in some way. On the other hand, I would be richer by two hundred dollars if it passed inspection. I wiped my eyes, consoling myself with that thought.

Then I remembered the Lotto number. If my marble really did possess the power to foretell the future, far more than two hundred dollars might prove to be my reward for setting it free.

Eagerly I awaited the evening of the next draw, fearful that Mitch would remain at home. But no. True to form, he went back to the lab. As I sat on the sofa in front of the TV, my ticket clutched in my hand, no one was there to lecture me about gullibility or explain that lotteries were a tax on the poor. When the Number 08-10-14-24-27-28 flashed onto the screen, no one was there to hear my shriek of joy.

The next day I opened an account in my own name at Royal Bank, depositing twenty dollars from my weekly housekeeping allowance.

"This isn't very much," I apologized to the teller, "but more is coming. Last night I won six million dollars from Lotto 649."

"Just a minute," said the teller, giving me a funny look. "I'll get somebody to talk to you."

She left me standing at the counter. I didn't blame her if she thought I was crazy. Perhaps I had been suffering from a massive delusion. But my lottery ticket was real, and it had the winning number printed right on it.

The teller returned with a man named Mr. Gibson, who introduced himself as my account manager, shook my hand, and led me into a small office. For half an hour he spoke to me in respectful tones about investment strategy. I recognized the words "NASDAQ" and "tech stocks". The rest was Greek to me.

"Mitch," I said as I cleared the table after dinner, "Sally Rockton wants me to go to Toronto with her tomorrow for a little shopping. I said I'd go, if that's all right."

"Sure." He pulled his wallet from his pants pocket, opened it and took out four fifty-dollar bills. "This came at the right time, eh? A little extra cash for your trip." As

I reached for it, his hand drew back. "Try not to spend it foolishly," he warned before releasing the money into my grasp.

In the morning I took the bus, afraid that I would become lost in Toronto if I tried to drive. I likely would have, because I had spent a mostly sleepless night and all day had the dazed feeling that I was living in a dream. I smiled for the photographer, drank champagne, and signed papers, all the time thinking, *When am I going to wake up?*

On the way home I sat clutching my purse – not the Gucci, which was still on my closet shelf. From time to time I peeked inside just to make sure that the documents the Lotto people had given me were still there. As the bus got closer to home, I began worrying about what to say to Mitch.

What tone should I take? Apologetic because I had done something he strongly disapproved of? Triumphant because I had won? And how should I begin? "Mitch, I've won six million in Lotto 649" did not sound promising. What about, "Mitch, we must talk"?

But he never gave me a chance to deliver any kind of opening line.

When I walked into the living room, he was sitting in his favourite chair, frowning severely. The *Journal of Applied Psychology* lay closed on his lap

"Sally Rockton phoned. She didn't seem to realize that she was in Toronto with you."

I sat down facing him. Straight in my chair. My back rigid. As his fingers steepled, I felt the cross-examination about to begin. That was the moment when I woke up

"I was in Toronto, Mitch. I was there to collect my lottery winnings. Six million dollars."

There was a minute of total silence. The steeple of his fingers collapsed.

"Seriously?" He looked stunned.

I nodded. "It's already in the bank."

"If this is true …" He gave me that superior little smile I knew so well. "That's a great deal of money for someone like you to manage."

"I'll invest it," I said. And it seemed as if a deep, hominoid voice called to me from far away. *"Watch NASDAQ. Tech stocks soar."*

Mitch and I "parted amicably", as they say. It's amazing how easily a thirty-five-year marriage can be undone. He claimed his half of the six million, which I suppose was fair, since he had supported me for so long.

I invested some of my three million in tech stocks, because it would have been impolite to disregard my marble's advice. After I had made a few thousand, Mr. Gibson got me out before the next slump, explaining that I'd be in a safer position with growth and investment funds.

I purchased a nice waterfront condominium with a balcony overlooking the bay. I also bought a new car and took my mother on a cruise. Seldom did I think about the marble that made it all possible.

Then one June evening I was sitting on my balcony browsing through the newspaper when my eye fell upon a story about the Queen's Plate. At first I thought it had something to do with royal dishes. As I read on, I learned that the Queen's Plate was the oldest continuously-run horse race in North America, and that it would take place in two days.

Something stirred in my brain.

Whoa! I thought, and looked for the names of the horses entered. Yes! There was Golden Boy. Odds: 150 to one.

Travelling by the Grand Bus Line

Mandy stood by the roadside sign, shivering in her quilted jacket and wondering whether she would freeze to death before the bus came by. Ever since the Schmidt General Store shut down ten years ago, there was no place to wait indoors. If you wanted to leave Schmidt and didn't have a car, you had to stand by the sign till the bus showed up. It passed through the village twice a day, heading south in the morning and north in the afternoon, stopping to pick up anyone who flagged it.

Pulling down the knitted cuff of her glove, Mandy checked her watch. Five minutes to three. She stamped her feet. They ached, but not so much as her stomach, where Phil had punched her. Her arms hurt from holding them up to shield her breasts. She tasted blood on the inside of her lips. Usually Phil was careful not to hit her face, not wanting his wife to walk around with visible bruises. He still had some pride. But yesterday he had driven into Swastika to pick up a part for his truck and stopped at the liquor store.

From where she stood, Mandy could keep an eye on their house, in case the front door opened. But Phil was asleep now. If the bus came soon, she would be far away when he woke.

The roadside sign, tilting from a snowbank, announced in faded letters:

SCHMIDT
Population 682

This number was not correct. It had not been correct for a long, long time.

Thirty years ago, when Mandy was a child, the business district had consisted of the Schmidt General Store, McDougall's Service Station, and Fred's Bait Shop. All boarded-up now. Thirty years before that, there had been a doctor's office, a post office and a poolroom. In its heyday in the 1890's, Schmidt had boasted a hotel with an assembly hall upstairs and a tavern downstairs. First a logging town, then a mining town, Schmidt was a ghost town now.

Or nearly a ghost town. There were still six inhabited houses, including the one where Phil and Mandy lived. Three were on the east side of the road, and three on the west, each separated from its nearest neighbour by at least one abandoned dwelling.

As Mandy waited, numbness crept into her feet. Her cheeks tingled with the first nip of frostbite. Her nostrils prickled. Her nose dripped. At least that wasn't frozen. She was wiping away the dribble with the back of her glove when, looking southward along the dark ribbon of asphalt, she spotted a moving object advancing between the banks of snow. As it drew nearer, the object became recognizable as a bus. A bright blue bus. Mandy picked up the brown Gladstone bag that sat in the snow by her feet, stepped forward onto the pavement, and waved. With a squeal of brakes, the bus slowed and stopped.

On its side, stencilled letters announced that this was the GRAND BUS LINE, an imposing title for a company whose entire fleet consisted of one vehicle. As it happened, "Grand" had been the name of the original owner. Tim Grand, a local man, had bought a used bus in 1949, seeing an opportunity to provide transportation for communities not on the railway. At intervals over the years, a newer used bus replaced its predecessor. The current vehicle was purchased when the North East District School Board retired it from service.

Its route covered seventeen villages and hamlets – ten linked by paved roads, the other seven by gravel. The bus's final stop was Kettle Lake. From there the traveller could catch the Northland bus to Timmins.

Timmins was Mandy's goal, though she wasn't sure she had enough money to travel that far. In Timmins, which was ten times bigger than Kettle Lake and one hundred times bigger than Schmidt, she would have a better chance of finding a job. Cleaning lady. Sales clerk. Waitress. Her skills were few.

In Timmins, it would be hard for Phil to find her.

When the door of the bus opened, Mandy hoisted the Gladstone aboard and then mounted the step.

"Cold day," the driver muttered.

"Sure is." Mandy opened her purse. "What's the fare?"

"You goin' as far as Kettle Lake?"

"Yeah."

"Twenty dollars."

She pulled out a twenty. That was a lot to pay just to get to Kettle Lake. She could forget about Timmins. Kettle Lake was as far as she could go.

Mandy sat down by a window, where somebody had left a newspaper on the empty seat. *The Kettle Lake Times.* January 29. That was the day before yesterday.

There were two headlines on the front page: "**Local family perishes in fire**" and "**No clues to murder victim's identity, Police say**".

Mandy decided to save the newspaper for later. She would be on the bus for three hours. Right now, all she wanted to do was relax and warm up. Too bad the seats didn't recline. She inhaled a long breath of stale air. In moments the last trace of Schmidt was behind her.

It was beginning. A new start. She had left Phil. After all the times she had wanted to, but didn't have the nerve, she was on her way.

Before leaving, she should have put more wood in the stove. The fire might burn out while Phil slept. Maybe she ought to phone him from Kettle Lake, just to be sure he was okay. She wouldn't need to tell him where she was.

She knew she should have left a note, but she never could get the spelling right.

After Phil woke up, it would take him a while to realize that she had left him. If he looked in the bedroom closet, he might notice that some of her clothes were missing, as well as his father's Gladstone bag, which had sat on the shelf for the past nine years, ever since Phil's father died.

Phil's father had been the last Schmidt to operate the general store.

Phil was the last Schmidt, period. End of the line. Mandy had given birth to twin daughters, stillborn, and in the process suffered medical complications that ended her reproductive years at age eighteen. Probably just as well, with Phil's drinking already out of hand.

At first his parents had objected to her as a possible daughter-in-law. They were the local big shots. Mandy's family was nothing. Mr. and Mrs. Schmidt originally had big plans for Phil. Wanting their only child to make something of himself and seeing no future in Schmidt, they had sent him to the University of Western Ontario to study Business Administration. At least, that was the program he had been registered in.

Mandy had left school at fourteen, after completing Grade Eight.

"No point you goin' on to high school," her father had said. "You pass easy for sixteen."

If she had registered for secondary school, the system would have caught her, because sixteen was the legal school-leaving age. By failing to register, Mandy slipped through a crack.

Mr. Schmidt gave her a job at the general store. After all, she did look sixteen – fully and voluptuously curved. Mr. Schmidt did not care for socialist nonsense like Minimum Wage, Social Insurance Numbers, Unemployment

Insurance, and the Canada Pension Plan. Mandy was the store's sole employee. He paid her straight from the till.

"Better for you this way," he told her, "so you don't have to pay Income Tax. One hundred and twenty dollars a week, and it's all yours."

Mandy thought this was pretty good pay. Her father let her keep twenty for herself.

Living in Schmidt, she had always known who Phil was. But until she started working at the store, Phil had never noticed her. The gap in their ages accounted for that; he was twenty the year she turned fourteen.

Phil was handsome, tall and blond, with hazel eyes and arched eyebrows that lifted expressively. When he was sober, his smile was very sweet.

She fell for him with total abandon, disregarding her mother's warning that no good would come of it. "He'll ruin you," Ma had said. "He'll chew you up and spit you out."

He certainly chewed her up, but he never spat her out.

Although Phil's father had no objection to his son sowing a few wild oats, Mrs. Schmidt had been unhappy about the whole affair. She spoke kindly to Mandy, advising her that it would be a big mistake to get "too friendly" with Phil. "Boys take liberties if they can; smart girls don't let them."

After Phil flunked first year for the second time, he did not return to Western. From then on, he hung around Schmidt, getting drunk and into the odd fight. His father barred him access to the store without actually accusing him of helping himself to cash from the till.

By the time Mandy turned seventeen, Phil's parents had changed their minds about her suitability. She was responsible. And she had an unquenchable desire to please. Maybe she could keep Phil in line. Nobody else could.

As a wedding present, the Schmidts gave the young couple a house. It had four rooms downstairs, and two up. Phil and Mandy had lived in this house for all twenty years of their marriage.

In 1992, the year his profits dropped to zero, Mr. Schmidt closed the store. Mandy went to work cleaning houses. Phil drove her into Swastika in the truck three times a week to the houses she cleaned.

Having nothing much to live for, Mr. Schmidt died the year after the store closed. Mrs. Schmidt soon followed. In their wills, the Schmidts had set up a trust to provide their hapless son with five hundred dollars a month for the rest of his life. It was not enough to live on. Mandy continued to clean houses.

Mandy picked up the newspaper from the seat beside her. As the bus bounced along, she read the story about the fire. Husband and wife, five children and a dog were now dead. An overheated wood stove was the cause. Flames sixty-five feet high. The fire truck arrived too late to save anything.

Mandy shuddered. That could happen to Phil, especially after a few drinks. You had to keep an eye on a wood fire. She folded the newspaper and set it back on the seat. Phil was not her responsibility. Not any longer. The taste of blood had gone from her mouth, but her stomach still hurt.

The bus stopped in one hamlet for a silent teenage boy wearing a backpack, and further along for an elderly woman with a large suitcase, who announced to all the bus that she was on her way to Kettle Lake to visit her daughter.

Later, the bus went by a car that had skidded into the ditch. The bus driver slowed down briefly, probably to check whether help was needed. Mandy had a good look. There was no one around. No driver. Just a grey Honda half overturned in the ditch.

The bus picked up the car's driver a few kilometres further, walking along the road. The shadows on the snow were long and blue, the way they become just before dark.

"Black ice," the motorist explained to the bus driver. "When the weather's real cold, it ices up bad along this stretch."

"Where's the nearest place I can hire a tow truck?"

"Kettle Lake. We'll be there in half an hour." He held out his hand. "Eight bucks."

At six o'clock, the bus arrived at its terminus, the parking lot of The Empress Hotel. Mandy and the stranded motorist were the only passengers to go inside. Everyone else got into one of the half-dozen cars that were waiting with their engines running.

As Mandy approached the desk in the lobby, the clerk looked up. She was a grey-haired woman with friendly eyes.

"May I help you?" she asked.

"I wonder if fifty dollars can get me a room for the night?"

The clerk looked at her sympathetically. "I'm afraid not."

"Is there someplace else I can try?"

"The Majestic. It's on Church Street. Three blocks left out the front door, then two right." She glanced at the worn Gladstone bag. "You can walk there, I think."

"First, I need to find a washroom."

"That way." The clerk pointed to a hall leading from the lobby. Mandy found the door marked LADIES. There were two toilet stalls, one with an out-of-order sign on the door.

As she opened the door to the other stall, she saw a black purse lying on its side on the floor, as if somebody had kicked it under the door.

She picked up the purse. Inside she found a packet of tissues, a makeup bag, and a wallet. No money in the wallet. No credit card. Whoever cleaned it out had left two things: a Social Insurance card and a Toronto Public Library card. Both bore the name Christine Bell.

Mandy had never had a library card or a Social Insurance Number. Maybe she should borrow these. She was about to start a new life, so why not start it with a new identity? Things were looking up. She wished she had thought to check her horoscope in that newspaper on the bus.

She put both the S.I.N. card and the library card into her own wallet. After returning Christine Bell's wallet to the purse, she dropped it behind the toilet.

As she walked the five blocks to the Majestic Hotel, Mandy practised saying her new name. Christine Bell. Christine Bell. Christine? Why not Chris? Or Chrissie? Yes. She would be Chrissie. It sounded friendly and cheerful.

The Majestic Hotel was a two-storey wooden building with a three-storey facade. Once-upon-a-time there had been a gallery, as evidenced by iron supports still bolted to the exterior wall. Taped to the window of the entrance door was a small sign: HELP WANTED.

Pushing open the door, Mandy stepped inside. The lobby's chief feature was a pool table. Four young guys were playing, setting down their beer bottles only to pick up their cues. They looked up as Mandy came through the door. Their gaze passed over her and dismissed her. They turned back to their game.

At the desk sat a thick-necked man, wearing a plaid shirt with the sleeves rolled up. The overhead light reflected off his bald scalp. He was watching a hockey game on a TV screen suspended from the ceiling.

"Yeah?" The man's eyes remained on the screen.

"I just got into town. I need a room for the night. I need a job, too. I seen the Help Wanted sign and I wonder, what kind of ...?"

Now he looked at her. "Chambermaid. Minimum wage. A free room comes with the job."

She took a quick breath. "I can clean rooms. Dust. Vacuum. Scrub floors. Make beds. I'm good at all that."

He eyed her closely. Maybe he noticed the swelling of her lip. Maybe it was her eagerness that grabbed his attention, the kind of eagerness that comes from desperation.

"You're hired."

He shoved a pad of paper and a pen across the desk. "Name. Social Insurance Number."

She pulled the card from her wallet and carefully wrote: Christine Bell. Then the nine-digit S.I.N. Gotta practise this, she thought.

He looked at her signature. "Christine Bell. Where have I heard that name before?"

"I go by Chrissie."

"I'm Art Smith. You can call me Art." He fished a key from a drawer behind the desk. "Room 205. Shared bathroom. You start work tomorrow. 8:00 a.m."

"Where can I get something to eat?"

"Try the Royal Café across the street."

Mandy found her room. The window overlooked the street. A row of long icicles, like spears, hung from the roof edge. She looked through their glistening brightness at the lighted sign of the Royal Café across the street. First she would unpack and settle in. Then go for a bite to eat.

An out-of-date calendar advertising Home Hardware was the only decoration in Mandy's room. There was a single bed, stripped to its blue-and-white mattress, with folded bedding stacked on top. The rest of the furniture consisted of a bedside table, a chest of drawers and a dresser with a cracked mirror. No telephone. There was a TV on a stand.

After taking off her outdoor clothing, she made the bed. Then she picked up the TV remote and lay down, a couple of pillows under her head, to relax for a few minutes. She had a room. She had a job. Her new life was starting out pretty good, she thought. Mandy clicked on the TV just as a newscast was starting. Her ears caught the first item:

The woman whose body was found behind the Kettle Lake Arena has been identified as Christine Bell of Toronto. The husband of the forty-two-year-old murder victim reported her missing five days ago.

Murder victim! The remote slipped from Mandy's fingers. This same item must have been on an earlier newscast. That's why Art Smith thought he'd heard the name before. She had stolen a dead woman's name.

If the police found out, she would be a suspect. She bowed her head, hands clasped, fighting down panic. "Help me, God," she prayed. "Dear God, please help me. I'll go back to Phil. I'll never run away again."

The wail of a siren submerged her prayer and the newscaster's voice. Mandy jumped up and looked out the window just as an Ontario Provincial Police cruiser, lights flashing, pulled up in front of the hotel. Two cops stepped out of the cruiser and headed toward the front door.

Mandy jumped away from the window, pulled on her boots and her jacket. Maybe there was a rear exit. Maybe she could get away.

Before she had her jacket zipped, footsteps sounded in the hall. A fist pounded on the door.

"Open up. This is the police."

Mandy cowered in a corner.

Art's voice. "You don't need to break down the door. I have a key."

A key clicked in the lock. The door opened. The two cops entered, guns drawn.

"Don't taser me!" she screamed.

"Take it easy, Ma'am," one officer said. "If you don't resist, you won't get hurt."

"I'm not really Christine Bell," she babbled as they cuffed her wrists behind her back.

"We know that. You can tell us the rest at the station."

Mandy sat on the edge of a bunk in a grey cell. The cell had a toilet and a sink. Bolts protruding from the cement-block wall above the sink showed where a mirror must have been. The cell smelled like Javex. It wasn't dirty, but it had a gritty look.

Bands of light spilled into her cell from the brightly-lit space outside the bars, where a policeman sat at a desk. He was staring at a computer screen. In front of him were a pad of yellow paper, a phone, and a coffee mug. He was a young man, his brown hair in a buzz cut.

This cop was not one of the two who had brought her in and questioned her earlier. Those men had frightened her so badly that her words tumbled all over each other when she tried to explain about the purse. At least she managed to give her real name, address and phone number.

After locking her up, they checked with the bus driver and with the desk clerk at the Empress Hotel. They phoned Phil. So they knew she could not be the person who dumped Christine Bell's body behind the Kettle Lake Arena. Mandy was in jail just because she had borrowed Christine Bell's ID. How was she supposed to know that was a crime?

The phone rang.

The officer at the desk picked it up. "Ontario Provincial Police. Kettle Lake Detachment."

As he listened to the caller, his eyes turned to Mandy.

"Schmidt. Is that right?" He wrote on the paper. "Philip. Yeah. We called him a couple of hours ago. He said he would drive here tonight."

Mandy leaned forward.

The officer still had his ear to the phone. "Yeah. Black ice is bad along that stretch. We've had a few land in the ditch. So where is he now?" A long pause. "Oh. I'll let her know." He hung up the phone.

She stared at him, wide-eyed.

"I'm sorry you have to hear it this way." A pause. "Your husband's truck skidded off the road and hit a tree. They've taken him to Kettle Lake Hospital. He's in the O.R. right now."

"Will he be all right?"

"He's critical. That's all the hospital will say."

Mandy turned her face to the wall.

"Mrs. Schmidt."

"Yes?"

"In the morning, before your court appearance, you can phone the hospital."

All night Mandy prayed that Phil would not die.

When she phoned the hospital in the morning, the surgeon who operated on Phil was still there. He told her that Phil's spinal cord had been severed in the lumbar region and his right arm crushed beyond saving. "He's lucky to be alive," the doctor said.

This was a lie. She should have prayed harder, or not at all.

The judge looked at her over his rimless glasses.

"Did it not occur to you that it was wrong to pass yourself off as somebody you are not?"

Mandy felt her face redden. "I never thought about that."

"Well, there's no law against stupidity. I find no evidence of criminal intent. Case dismissed."

A man wearing a black robe said, "All upstanding."

Everybody stood. The judge walked out a door behind the bench.

"What happens now?" Mandy asked the officer escorting her.

"Nothing. You're free."

She looked at him blankly. Free to do what? Free to go where?

"If you want, I can give you a lift to the hospital."

Mandy nodded. And then she was walking behind him down a hall, looking at the gun in the holster at his side.

At the hospital, a doctor met her outside the nursing station.

"You must be prepared for any outcome," he told her. "Your husband could die within the next few hours, or he could live for years. It's too soon to tell. If he makes good progress, you'll even be able to take him home."

"You mean he'll get better?"

"Not exactly. As a paraplegic, he'll require permanent, constant care."

Mandy could not speak. Phil's terrible accident was all her fault. It wouldn't have happened if she hadn't run away.

"When you feel ready to see your husband, ask at the nursing station. A nurse will take you to his room."

When the doctor left, Mandy walked to a nearby bench and sat down. She stared at the opposite wall. She felt numb. It seemed that her lot in life was to take care of Phil. It started out that way, and that's the way it would always be.

A woman approached. An older woman. Not a nurse. Her badge said "Volunteer".

"May I get you a cup of tea?"

A cup of tea. Mandy's mind fastened onto the idea. Did she want a cup of tea?

The volunteer waited patiently. Mandy said yes.

"How do you take it?"

Take it? In that question, she heard her mother's voice. "Mandy, I don't know how you take it." Mom wanted her to leave Phil. She'd seen the awkward way Mandy held herself the time her ribs were cracked. "He doesn't mean it." Mandy had tried to defend her man. "He's only like that when he's had too much to drink." But it seemed he was always like that now. Mandy couldn't remember the last time she saw the sweet smile that melted her heart. She couldn't recall the exact moment when she knew that she had had enough.

The volunteer's voice broke through Mandy's thoughts. "Do you take milk and sugar?"

"Yes. Milk and sugar. Please."

When she had finished her cup of tea, a nurse took charge and led her to Phil's room.

There were two beds in the room. One was empty. The other held Phil, swathed in bandages and hooked up with tubes. Various containers of clear liquids were suspended over his head. His right arm ended above the elbow in a bandaged stump. He lay utterly still. The only movement was his chest, moving up and down.

"Sit down," the nurse said. "He's asleep. The anaesthetic has worn off. When he wakes up, he'll want you here." The nurse left her alone with Phil.

Watching him, Mandy felt trapped. Maybe God had done this on purpose to keep her from leaving Phil. Her emotions churned, and she seethed with mingled anger and guilt. Beneath everything, there was love. She couldn't get over that.

With one ear she heard buzzing sounds and low voices from the nursing station. In the hallway something went by, a gentle rumbling like a suitcase on wheels. Mandy sat on the edge of the bed. She wanted to hold Phil's hand, but he had only one, and it was tied down to prevent him from dislodging the tube that entered his arm at the crook of his elbow. There were tubes coming out his nose, too. Mandy settled for stroking his hair.

His eyes opened and his eyebrows lifted. He licked his lips.

"Hi, Mandy." Then came the smile that always melted her heart. "I was worried about you. I knocked at every door. Somebody saw you waiting for the bus." He paused. "I couldn't figure out … what was going on."

This speech seemed to exhaust him. His eyes were on her, as if he was waiting for an explanation.

With a start, she realized that he had not known she was leaving him. He hadn't noticed anything missing, not even his father's Gladstone bag. He didn't know, and she would never tell him. She would take him home. She would care for him. They would never part.

He spoke again, his voice husky.

"Mandy, get me a drink."

"Water?"

"No. I mean a real drink. Scotch … rye … rum. Anything."

She pulled back. It was on her lips to say no. He wanted the very thing that had destroyed his life. She looked up at the bags suspended overhead. His painkillers. His medicines. His nourishment. She looked at his legs that would never move again. She looked at the stump of his right arm.

"Please." There was that smile again. "It's the last thing I'll ever ask you to do for me."

It's an amazing world we live in, Mandy thought as she looked out the bus window. It didn't matter what we plan. Life always seemed to work out some way that was different. Here she was travelling the Grand Bus Line back to Schmidt, which was the place where she belonged. In the Gladstone bag was an urn containing Phil's ashes, returning to the place where he belonged, too. In the spring his ashes would be buried in the Schmidt family plot, where his ancestors from way back two hundred years lay buried. It was a large plot, enclosed by an iron fence, with a big stone angel in the middle and gravestones all around. Phil would be safe there. She would visit every Sunday.

Mandy had no money. But she realized that now she would own the house, as well as the boarded-up general store. Maybe she could open it again. Not as a store. As a diner it might be successful. Lots of tourists travelled that road during summer. Then deer hunters came in the fall. Mandy was a hard worker, and she made good pies.

The Errand

The houses on this block were old but nicely kept. Shrubs and flowers. Green squares of lawn. Fiona parked her car in front of Number 79. It was a red-brick house with a blue porch. In one of the front windows was a hand-lettered sign: "Room for Rent".

Across the street an old man was feeding pigeons. He stood on the grassy strip between the sidewalk and the pavement, sprinkling seeds from an open plastic bag. Pigeons surrounded him, strutting pompously on their pink feet and bobbing to pick up grain. Watching the old man and the pigeons, Fiona recalled that there was a bylaw against feeding birds. Until her illness, her grandmother had fed pigeons, too. The bylaw hadn't stopped Grandma. She had always been a bit of a rebel.

Fiona sat for a moment considering what to say to whoever came to the door of Number 79. Then, her heart pounding, she got out of the car, approached the house, and climbed the porch steps. Pausing in front of the door, she lifted her finger to press the doorbell.

Until the bell was pressed, she still had the option of leaving, for there was nothing to stop her from running to the car and driving away. But having come this far, it would be cowardly to turn back. She thought of Grandma, propped on pillows, her body wasted by cancer, her mind fogged by morphine. Yet she had been clear about the ring.

It was an amber ring that a Polish airman stationed in Hamilton during World War II had given her when she was seventeen. He had told her that amber was Poland's most famous gem and that someday he would take her to his homeland. Theirs was a secret engagement. She had kept the ring hidden under an attic floorboard. When her parents sent her away, she had not had time to retrieve the ring. Now, as her life neared its end, she wanted the ring. She asked for nothing else. She had given Fiona a crude drawing to help her find it.

Fiona had known about the airman since the age of fifteen, when her grandmother deemed her mature enough to understand "matters of the heart". If he had not been killed on a bombing mission, Grandma would have become Mrs. Pilsudski. Mrs. Boleslaw Pilsudski. And Fiona might be living in Poland. Except she wouldn't be Fiona. She would be Hedwig, or something else strange like that.

Grandma's parents had opposed the match. That the airman was a Catholic was bad, that he was a Pole – a foreigner – made it worse. With those black marks against him, he was not welcome in their home. They had ordered their daughter to stay away from him. But she was in love and did not obey.

Fiona's mother did not know about the ring. Every time Grandma started to reminisce about her Polish airman, Fiona's mother would press her lips together and leave the room. Illegitimacy was the cross she had to bear. She never forgave Grandma for inflicting that stigma upon her.

Fiona suspected that her mother was a throwback to the hard, cruel, unfeeling parents who had sent away their own daughter, who was only seventeen, because she had been too generous in her love.

Everybody knew that Fiona's mother was married, even though her husband had run off many years ago. She called herself Mrs. Morris (never Ms.) and wore a wedding ring. Fiona had never blamed her father for leaving her mother, who was an angry woman. Her nature was cold and unloving. If it weren't for Grandma, Fiona would have left home as soon as she was old enough.

All she remembered of her father was the smell of cigarettes and a sandpapery cheek that she kissed. As a child, she had liked to think that he would come for her some day, though she had no idea where he would take her or what their life together would be like. Now twenty years old, she had abandoned this dream, although she still hoped that someday he would try to get in touch with her. Fiona's mother did not know where he was, but thought it might be Australia. If that was the case, Fiona might as well forget about seeing him again.

Fiona rang the bell. Heavy footsteps sounded on the other side of the door. There was a pause. She assumed that someone was inspecting her through the peephole.

The man who opened the door had a beer belly, grey hair and bushy eyebrows.

Fiona cleared her throat. "I'm sorry to disturb you. My grandmother used to live here. She wants me to find something she left behind. A ring. She left home in a hurry. She didn't have time ..."

"Miss, I've lived in this house for thirty years. You got the wrong place."

He started to close the door.

"No! Wait!" She pushed her palm against the door. "It was a very long time ago. 1941. I'm sure this is the right address. I know where to look."

"Where?"

"The ring is hidden under ..." Fiona caught herself in time.

The man gave an embarrassed, caught-in-the-act sort of laugh, followed by a frown. "You're telling me you want into my house to look for a ring your grandmother left here sixty years ago? If there was such a ring, it changed hands along with the house. Forget it!"

The door closed.

Across the street, the old man was still feeding the pigeons. He looked about the same age as Grandma. In this settled, working-class part of town, many families stayed in the same house from generation to generation. There was a chance that the old man had lived here all his life, and in that case he might have known Fiona's grandmother long ago.

Instead of returning to her car, Fiona crossed the street. She had no plan. She didn't expect that the old man would be able to help her. What she felt was mostly curiosity. She had never met anyone who had known her grandmother as a girl.

The old man was thin and stooped. He wore dark worsted trousers held up by both suspenders and a belt. Above the belt was a red plaid shirt, fully buttoned, and worn with a string tie. His hair was white, and his face clean-shaven. His hands were large and gnarled.

"Nice afternoon for feeding birds," she said.

"Indeed it is." He smiled as if glad to have someone to talk to.

"This is a nice neighbourhood." Fiona felt her face flush with the embarrassment she always felt when speaking to a stranger. "Have you lived here a long time?"

With a slight movement of his free hand, he indicated the narrow brick house at his back. "My parents bought this place in 1928. I grew up here."

"Then you might have known a girl named Agnes Calder? She lived across the street."

He looked at the house with the blue porch.

"Yes. I knew her."

"She's my grandmother."

"Don't tell me Agnes is still alive!" His eyes brightened. Fiona nodded.

"Her family moved here when I was fourteen," the old man said. "Agnes must have been sixteen. Anyway, she was two grades ahead of me in school. Prettiest girl at Central Collegiate. I don't suppose she remembers me."

"I guess you know what happened to her?"

"Oh, yes. She got too friendly with one of those Polish flyers who trained in Hamilton during the war. Everybody knew about it. She dropped out of school and went away. I never saw her again."

"Her parents sent her to a home for pregnant girls. She kept the baby. That's my mother."

He nodded. "I've wondered since then what happened to her. Did she ever get married?"

"No. She came close to it once, she told me. Then the man's older sister talked him out of it; she asked him if he really wanted to bring up another man's child."

"Maybe she was lucky he bailed out." The old man tossed another handful of seeds to the birds. "I was married fifty years. My missus and I raised five kids in this house. Two boys and three girls. They're scattered all across the country." He turned the plastic bag upside down and shook it. A few grains spilled out. "That's all you get today," he said to the pigeons.

"My grandmother used to feed the birds. I was thinking about her when I saw you."

He smiled. "Maybe you'd like a cup of tea. My name is Alvin Liebrock."

She returned his smile. "I'm Fiona Morris. And I would love a cup of tea."

Alvin Liebrock seemed exactly the sort of grandfather she would like to have. Soon after her father abandoned his family, all contact with her Morris grandparents had ceased. And she never thought of the Polish airman as a grandfather. Seen through Grandma's eyes, he was forever young.

Alvin's house was nearly identical to the one across the street. A border of marigolds across the front. Five steps up to a wooden porch. He held the door for her to enter.

The front-hall wallpaper bore a pattern of flowers and leaves, badly faded except for three pronounced rectangles where deep maroon and varied shades of green showed what the colours used to be. A single nail hole marked each rectangle. He has taken down his pictures, Fiona thought, and wondered why.

"The kitchen is that way." He pointed to the back of the house.

In the small kitchen were a stove, a refrigerator and an old-fashioned enamelled sink. The kitchen was very neat, with not so much as a dirty coffee mug sitting on the counter. A white table stood at the window, with three wooden chairs. There were no curtains on the window, although there were brackets to hold a curtain rod.

"Have a seat," Alvin said. "I'll put on the kettle."

At first she did not sit, but stood at the window looking out at the neatly-mowed patch of grass and at the masses of rose bushes that surrounded it.

"I like roses," Fiona said. "And you have such a lot!"

He joined her at the window.

"They've been growing wild for a year since my wife died. I need to prune them, but I'm not sure how. That was something she always did."

By the time they sat down facing each other with the teacups in front of them, Fiona knew that she was going to tell him about the amber ring. Yet her tea was half drunk before she began, hardly lifting her eyes above the rim of the cup.

"The reason I stopped by was to ask the man across the street if I could look for a ring that my grandmother hid under the floorboards in the attic. Her fiancé gave it to her."

"The Polish airman?"

She nodded. "They would have married, but she was underage and her parents wouldn't give permission. She didn't know she was pregnant until he'd been sent overseas. Then he was killed in action. His name was Boleslaw Pilsudski. She called him Bobby. For some reason, she never had a chance to retrieve the ring before her parents sent her away.

"For a couple of years she was estranged from her mother and father because she refused to give up her baby for adoption. Eventually there was a reconciliation, but by then her parents had sold the house and moved.

"My grandmother is dying. She talks about Bobby all the time, and about the ring." Fiona set down her cup. "Last wishes are usually about something to be done after the person dies. So this is different. She wants the ring back while she's still alive." Fiona sighed. "I asked the man who lives there now if I could look for the ring. He told me to forget it, and he shut the door in my face."

"That sounds like Bill. He can be gruff. But, in fairness to him, I doubt many people would let a stranger into their house to look around."

"I suppose not."

"If he let you in, would you know where to look?"

Fiona opened her handbag and pulled out a used envelope. There was a clumsy sketch on the back.

"Grandma drew this to show me where to look. I'm afraid it's not very clear. Her hands are shaky." Alvin took the sketch from her.

"This is clear enough. It looks as though the attic floorboards don't reach all the way from wall to wall. There isn't a complete floor. More like a platform at the top of the stairs. The attic in my house was like that before I finished it to make an extra bedroom."

"Grandma said I'd just have to reach under the floorboards. You see how the spot is marked with an X? The ring is in a white glove."

Alvin looked up. "May I borrow this? I have an idea." He must have seen her hesitation. "Don't worry. I won't try to break in."

"You really think you can get the ring?"

"Unless the attic has been renovated, it should still be there." His eyes met hers. "Let me try. I liked Agnes very much, you see."

Fiona nodded slowly. Long ago, Alvin had liked the girl who later would become her grandmother. Didn't that create some sort of link between them? Not exactly a family connection. But sort of like that.

"All right. Maybe you'll have better luck than I did." Fiona checked her watch. Two minutes to four. "Time to go. I start work in twenty minutes." She pushed back her chair from the table. "Thanks for the tea."

He stood. "Give me a week."

Alvin walked her to the door.

Fiona was a university student. She had found summer employment with a dry cleaning business. The firm had three outlets. Her job was to work at the counter of one store or another while regular staff took holidays. She found time to visit her grandmother every day.

Her grandmother's room at the hospice was airy and sunny, with a picture window overlooking a garden. The walls were peach-pink, and on them hung framed pictures brought from home. Three were of Fiona at various stages of growing up.

Grandma, propped up in her steel-sided bed, turned her head at Fiona's entrance. Fiona kissed her cheek, lowered the side of the bed, and pulled a chair very close. When she took her grandmother's hand, the fingers closed around hers like a baby's reflex.

"Grandma, I'm so sorry, but I don't have the ring. The man who owns the house wouldn't let me in to look for it."

The old woman squeezed Fiona's hand. "At least you tried."

"But while I was there – across the street, actually – I met someone you may remember. Alvin Liebrock."

"Alvin Liebrock! Is he still alive?"

Did old people always ask this question? It seemed so sad.

"Yes. He was feeding pigeons."

"That sounds like Alvin. He was a nice boy. He lived right across the street."

"He still does. He told me you were the prettiest girl at Central Collegiate."

"Did he say that?" She smiled.

Fiona decided not to mention Alvin's quest. He was no more likely to recover the ring than she had been. Why risk another disappointment?

"My life would have been different if I had fallen in love with a boy like Alvin," Fiona's grandmother said. "Of course, he was a couple of years too young for me to think of in that way. I was very romantic when I was seventeen. During the war, all of us girls were romantic. If we weren't in love with the serviceman, we were in love with his uniform. Nothing is more romantic than to give yourself to a hero who's almost doomed to die."

Fiona, who had not yet given herself to anyone, leaned closer, eager to hear.

"I met Bobby at a dance. When I first saw him, I thought he was in the Royal Canadian Air Force. But when he turned sideways, I saw 'Poland' on his shoulder badge. The Polish airmen training in Hamilton wore the same uniforms as the RCAF.

"He introduced himself, gave a little bow, and asked me to dance. His eyes were bluish grey, the same shade as his uniform." She smiled again. "We had six wonderful weeks.

Then he went overseas." Tears began to run through the creases of her cheeks. "I never saw him again, but not a day passed without me thinking about him."

The old woman fell silent, and Fiona knew that she was unlikely to hear more; her grandmother seemed to have dropped a curtain over her memories.

"Are you tired?"

"A little."

"I'll go then." Fiona kissed her forehead.

"Don't feel bad about the ring. I would've liked it, but I'll see Bobby soon."

"Yes." Tears filled Fiona's eyes. "It won't be long before you're with him again."

Nearly every day Fiona drove by Alvin Liebrock's house. She did not see him. But she noticed that the "Room for Rent" sign was no longer in the window of the house across the street.

After a week, she dropped by, as he had suggested, in order to find out whether he had succeeded in retrieving the ring. Even before she reached the front door, she felt that something was wrong. She put her finger to the bell and rang it. No one came.

It was then that she looked through the front windows into the living room. Paint-spotted drop sheets covered the floor. Empty paint cans were stacked in one corner. A stepladder stood in the middle of the room.

He's gone, she thought. Something had happened to Alvin. They – meaning his children – were readying his house to put it on the market. Soon a "For Sale" sign would appear on the front lawn. She had lost her only chance to recover the ring. Not only that, but she would never see him again. She knew it was ridiculous to feel such a rush of sadness about someone whom she had met only once, but she couldn't help it.

Two days later, she was again driving by when she saw him standing on the sidewalk, pigeons clustered about his feet. She pulled over to the curb and got out. As she approached him, she had to resist the temptation to give him a hug.

"Good news!" Alvin said. "I have the ring. I'll tell you all about it while we have a cup of tea." He tossed one more handful of seeds to the birds and then tied the top of the bag.

As soon as they entered the house, Fiona saw that the faded wallpaper in the front hall had been replaced by fresh paint. Framed pictures hung in the places where empty rectangles had been. Alvin motioned her into the kitchen, which also gleamed with new paint.

"I've been staying across the street," Alvin put on the kettle. "Bill had a room for rent."

"I saw the sign in the window."

"That's what gave me my idea for getting back the ring. If I could rent that room, I'd be Johnny-on-the-spot. So I went over to talk to Bill. I'd already hired painters to do the whole inside of my house. I knew it was time to brighten the place up, and I'm too old for climbing ladders." Alvin opened a tea canister. "I'd planned to stay put during the painting – just move from room to room to keep out of the way. I'd sleep in whatever bedroom the painters had finished or hadn't started yet. But now I saw how I could get into Bill's house without causing suspicion. I told him I wanted to rent his room for a week till the painters were finished."

"I'm surprised he'd be willing to rent it to someone for just one week."

"I pointed out he wouldn't likely find a long-term tenant until the college students came back in September, so he might as well let me rent it. Bill knew this was true. So I packed a suitcase and moved across the street.

"I thought Bill was never going to leave the house. I sat in that rented room, reading magazines, for nearly the whole week before he told me he had to go grocery shopping. As soon as he drove off, I nipped up to the attic. It took me two minutes to find the ring, right where the sketch showed it would be. It was shoved into the finger of a glove, though the colour sure wasn't white any longer."

Alvin lifted the kettle from the stove and filled the teapot. "I'll fetch it while the tea steeps."

He shuffled off to a different room. When he returned, he was carrying a filthy glove, darkened with grime. He held it with the fingers hanging down, like a severed hand.

Rather than reach inside, Fiona held the glove upside down by two fingertips. The ring fell onto the table.

After being wiped with a tissue, the amber glowed with a warm clear light. On impulse she slipped the ring onto her own third finger, left hand. Turning her hand from side to side, admiring the ring, she imagined Agnes Calder doing the same thing.

"I'll take it to my grandmother as soon as we've finished our tea."

"May I go with you? I want to see her again."

"Oh! Do you think you should? She's so frail. They give her morphine every four hours. And she's shrunk to nearly nothing. Eighty-five pounds. Wouldn't you rather remember her as she was, the prettiest girl at Central Collegiate?"

"I shan't have any trouble remembering that."

They looked at each other.

"Then you give her the ring," said Fiona. "You're the one who found it."

They drank their tea in silence. Alvin pushed back his chair. "Give me five minutes to change my clothes."

She did not object, although she thought he looked fine in his plaid shirt and dark pants.

He returned wearing a dark grey suit, white shirt, and red bow tie. The suit sagged upon his bony frame. His white hair was combed neatly into place.

He's dressed for a date, Fiona thought.

When they reached the hospice, Fiona left Alvin waiting in the hall, the door open. A nurse was in the room, busy attaching a sort of patch to the old woman's right arm, close to the shoulder.

"What's that?" Fiona asked.

"It's called a butterfly. By using this we can administer morphine as often as she needs without having to jab her every time."

The wizened figure on the bed turned her head slowly. She smiled at Fiona. "It's wonderful! No more pain. I feel like a butterfly." Her voice was barely audible. "It makes me float."

"The morphine slows her breathing. She'll tire quickly," the nurse said before leaving the room.

Fiona bent over the bed to hug the frail patient, embracing her as gently as if she were made of tissue paper. She laid her smooth cheek against her grandmother's withered cheek.

"I've brought someone to see you. He has your ring. He wants to give it to you himself."

Straightening up, she beckoned to Alvin. He stepped into the room, holding the amber ring between his thumb and forefinger.

The old woman's mouth stretched wide in a smile. Slowly she raised her left hand for him to slip the ring onto her finger.

"Bobby! I've been waiting for you."

"It's the morphine," Fiona said. "She thinks –"

"Let it be."

Alvin held Agnes Calder's hand.

Patchwork Pieces
[A Quartet]

*

"The Quilt"
"The Legacy"
"The Auction"
"RIP"

The Quilt

When Judy came over today, she brought me a new mohair throw. "There," she said, "this will keep you a lot warmer than that old quilt you've been using." She tucked it around my legs. I stroked the soft, silky wool. Light as a feather and very pretty – deep rose and dark green. I like those colours.

Knowing Judy, there had to be something behind it. Everything she does for me is for my own good, of course, and I'm lucky to have a daughter who cares. But all the time I wonder what she's up to.

She thinks I don't notice, but – merciful heavens – does she imagine that my mind is as weak as my legs? Judy is forever giving me advice on how to handle my own affairs. Selling my house was her idea. I don't deny that it made sense.

"Mom," she said, "you're eighty years old and you live alone. You don't need four bedrooms, three bathrooms and half an acre of lawn that has to be mowed every week."

"Maybe you're right," I said. "It doesn't make much sense, does it?"

Yet I did love the house. It had meant so much to Bill. That's why I held on to it for twenty years after he died. The house was his pride and joy. It showed the world how far he'd come.

When Bill was a boy, nobody around Hay Bay had indoor plumbing. Backhouse behind the kitchen garden. Chamber pot under the bed. When Bill gave visitors a house tour, those three bathrooms were the star attraction.

"Of course I'm right." Judy put on that tight, self-satisfied smile. "Keeping the house must cost you a fortune. Taxes. Insurance. Heating. And what do you pay the man who cuts the grass?"

That was Judy. Prying, prying. Digging into my finances. Why did she need to know how I spent every penny? Did she think I wasn't competent? Or was she worried about me spending her inheritance?

But she was right about selling the house. The timing was good, too. Five years later, I wouldn't have got two hundred and fifty thousand. That's two hundred and fifty thousand net, after commission and legal fees. A lot more than it would fetch in today's market. I was glad to get the house off my hands. All I need is a one-bedroom apartment. And my quilt.

Where did Judy put my quilt? There aren't a lot of places where it could vanish.

"That quilt is my book of memories," I'd told Judy many a time. Better than old photograph albums. Snapshots are only grey and white images – at least the snapshots I care about are grey and white – showing one single moment. Well, I guess that's the idea, isn't it? Snap! You shoot the moment. Capture it, dead or alive, on a shiny rectangle of paper.

Ah, but a quilt! Every patch of fabric tells a story. Take the grey flannel squares. Bill's good suit. He bought that when they elected him reeve. Bill needed something nice to wear to township council meetings. He wore it for a long time, until it got too tight. The Jessop men always got heavy. First they got fat, then they got bald, and then they got a heart attack. Why had I thought that Bill would be an exception? He was sixty-two when he died. That was more than twenty years ago.

I still miss that dear, sweet man! I touch those grey flannel squares and feel Bill in his suit. Big shoulders. Strong arms to hold me. Well, I'm not going to dwell on it.

Then there are the navy blue squares. Tim's blazer. Wasn't he the handsome fellow in that! We bought him the blazer for his high school graduation. It cost a bundle, but Tim said he would be able wear it to dances at university, and to weddings. Brand new when I cut it up for squares. He wore it once.

Oh, where is my quilt?

Judy keeps reading those articles about coping with elderly parents: "Choosing a Retirement Home", "Best Buys in Planned Funerals", "When to Get Power of Attorney", and "Is Revenue Canada Your Heir?"

I read them too, but I don't tell her. I have to keep ahead of Judy somehow. Sit down with your old father/mother, they say. Be tactful but frank.

Judy tried it. "Mom, maybe it's time for you to tell me about your assets."

"What assets?' I pretended not to understand. "Do you mean my big brown eyes?"

"No!"

"My intelligence, then?"

"Oh, stop it," she said. "You know perfectly well what I mean. Bank accounts. Investments. Where's your safety deposit box? I should know where things are in case something happens to you."

"What exactly do you have in mind?" I asked her. "Are you planning for something to happen?" Judy backed off. She could never bring herself to use the word 'death'. Not to me, anyhow. I felt sorry for her, she looked so embarrassed.

The navy blue squares break my heart. Bill said not to use them, but I wasn't going to throw away my last good memory of Tim. All the other kids had got out of the car before the train hit. Stalled on the tracks. Tim was sure he could get it started. That's what his friends said. He didn't want to wreck his dad's car. As if the damn car was worth Tim's life. Something was wrong with the carburetor. That car was always stalling. Bill should have traded it in long before.

I can touch the navy blue squares and see Tim up there on the stage receiving his scholarship. Curly black hair. Broad shoulders like his dad's. Best-looking boy in the graduating class. Bill and I sat in the front row of the auditorium. Judy may have been with us, but I'm not sure. Bill was bursting with pride to see his son shake hands with Mr. Fletcher, the Chairman of the School Board. "Congratulations," Mr. Fletcher said when he handed Tim the envelope. "You're a credit to Hay Bay."

As Tim turned to leave the stage, he looked at me and smiled.

Afterwards, we sat around the kitchen table and ate the cake that I had baked and decorated with "Congratulations Tim!" in chocolate icing. That's the last cake I ever decorated. Judy wanted me to do her wedding cake. Maybe I should have, but I couldn't work up enough enthusiasm.

Tim read the award letter to us. Four years free tuition at the University of Toronto, plus five thousand dollars cash. That's pretty good for a farm boy whose parents left school at sixteen. It's a shame Tim never got to use his scholarship. He wanted to be a doctor.

I can touch the navy blue squares and remember Tim the way he was at eighteen. At least, I could touch them if I had the quilt here on my lap. It's not in the linen cupboard. It's not on my bed. I certainly hope that Judy hasn't put it in the wash. She has good intentions, but sometimes I wish that she would leave well enough alone.

It was thirty years ago that I made the quilt. We were still on the farm – that was before we sold out to the developer and bought the house in Napanee. I had the squares all pieced together and ready to quilt, when I said to Bill, "I'm going to have an old-fashioned quilting bee, like my mother used to. There are women around here who haven't been to a quilting bee since they were girls."

"Good idea," Bill said. He was still reeve then, before his second heart attack. Bit of a glad-hander, Bill was, always thinking about the next election. "Be sure to let the newspaper know about it so they can send a photographer."

Sure enough, the *Napanee Beaver* showed up to take a picture of us ladies. I still have that picture in a shoebox somewhere. The newsprint was yellow and falling apart last time I looked at it.

Bill fetched my quilting frame from the attic. He'd made it for me when we were first married, and was very proud of it.

"We'll set it up in the kitchen," I said.

So we pushed the table aside to make room for the frame, and then put out chairs all along the sides. Before the women arrived, Bill and I had attached the pieced-together squares to the frame, with the cotton batting to line it, and then the backing. The backing was dark red, a lovely warm colour.

There were eight women, some of them neighbours and others from the church that Bill and I attended. Not one was under forty years old. Even thirty years ago, young women didn't do quilting. Everything store-bought. Judy couldn't do a decent quilting stitch to save her life.

We chatted the whole time – talked about recipes and who'd had a baby and who'd died. Stitch, stitch, stitch all day long. When we had finished quilting, we tidied everything up and served the sandwiches and pies that the women had brought with them. I put the big kettle on the stove to make tea for everybody.

I was happy that day. My fingers were sore, but I was truly happy.

A few weeks later Judy saw the quilt when she came home for the weekend. Judy worked in an office in Kingston. She was about twenty at the time, finished school. Never went to college. In this family, Tim had all the brains as well as the good looks.

When she looked at the quilt her eyes narrowed. "Why aren't there any squares for me?" There was that chip on her shoulder, as usual.

"Oh, there must be," I said.

"Not one."

When I took a good look, I saw that she was right. "Well," I said, "I guess there weren't any old clothes of yours in the scrap bag. No need to take on about it."

It was like Judy to make something out of nothing. She never did appreciate that quilt.

We sold the farm the year after that. The developer paid a good price. One hundred thousand dollars looked like a fortune in 1972. Bill thought he'd struck gold. But I realize now that if we'd waited a few years, we could have got a million for two hundred acres with half-a-mile of Lake Ontario shoreline. After selling the farm, we moved to Napanee and bought the big house. Bill died two years later.

Judy wanted me to buy a condominium after I sold the house in Napanee.

"No," I said. "I don't want to own any more property. I'm going to rent an apartment until I'm ready to check into a retirement home. And I don't need any help in finding what I want."

Judy spluttered a bit. She always wants to put her oar in. "There's not much to choose from in Napanee."

"Who says it has to be Napanee? I'm moving to the big city."

She turned pale. "Toronto?"

"No. Kingston."

She looked relieved. "That's good," she said. "It will be easy for me to drop in a couple of times a week to check on you. I can take you shopping and to doctor's appointments."

I felt like saying I was still capable of driving myself, but that would have started a row. Judy needs to feel useful. Fifty years old. Married. No kids. Not enough to occupy her time.

You should have seen her face when she saw the apartment. Uniformed doorman. Oil paintings in the lobby. Every luxury known to man. "Mom, you can't afford this!" she said.

"Oh, can't I?"

I had never told her what I got for the house, but I'm pretty sure she found out somehow.

"Put the money from selling the house into Guaranteed Investment Certificates," had been her advice. "Then your capital will be safe, and you can live comfortably on the interest."

Well, I didn't want to live comfortably. For the first time in my life, I wanted to live in style.

If Judy knew that I'd put two hundred thousand into a Guaranteed Single Life Annuity! Well, I don't know what she'd say. For the rest of my life, $2,168 goes automatically into my bank account every month. That's double what I would have got from those GIC's she wanted me to buy. Of course, the money dies with me. At my death the insurance company keeps the capital. Nothing left for Judy.

It isn't as if she'll ever really be in need. Judy has a husband to support her. And she'll still get the fifty thousand I've sewn into the quilt. All in one-thousand-dollar bills. They were crisp and new when I got them from the bank. I wore them inside my brassiere for a week to soften them up. Twenty-five on each side. *Lily Jessop,* I said to myself, *you have a fifty-thousand-dollar bosom! I bet even Mae West can't beat that.*

I sewed the money into the quilt five years ago when Judy was complaining about the backing looking all shabby and worn. "Buy me the fabric," I said, "and I'll put on a new backing." So she did. Dark blue. It looked really nice. The same shade as the quilt squares from my old plaid skirt. That was a lovely skirt. I used to wear it when I went for walks with Bill … when I could walk. A long time ago.

You know, I hate to say this, but I'm afraid that I've seen the last of my quilt. I think that Judy tossed it out when she gave me this store-bought throw. A few days ago, she was making nasty comments about my quilt. Said it was only fit for the garbage. Oh, yes. She would do that. Judy doesn't like old things.

The Legacy

The lawyer, Mr. Lloyd, was very tall, and he bowed his bald head as he asked Judy to come into his office. He held the door open for her and, when he had closed it, directed her to the chair placed in front of his desk. It was a button-back chair, upholstered in red leather so dark it appeared almost black. It looked expensive. Everything in Mr. Lloyd's office looked expensive. As she sat down, Judy felt acutely aware that her pink, ultra-suede pantsuit with the wide lapels was ten years out of style.

Mr. Lloyd sat down behind his desk in a chair that matched the one where he had seated her, but his was larger and more majestic.

"Mrs. Aylesworth, there's nothing complicated about your mother's will." He looked down at the document on his desk. "You are the sole executor – I should say, executrix – of the estate of Lily Catherine Jessop and, except for a few small bequests, the sole beneficiary."

Judy let out a sigh of relief. She had been afraid that her mother would leave a big legacy to Saint Alban's Church, which was a threat she had made from time to time to keep her daughter in line.

"To carry out your responsibilities as executrix will not be onerous." His voice was grave and reassuring. "Your mother's estate is very small."

Small? Not by my standards, Judy thought. From the look of his office, Mr. Lloyd was accustomed to dealing with billion-dollar estates. To him, one-quarter of a million might seem a pittance. To her, it was a windfall.

Mr. Lloyd continued. "The entire estate consists of the balance in your mother's bank account, a little over three thousand dollars –"

"What!" Judy sat bolt upright.

"Let me continue." Mr. Lloyd raised his hand in polite remonstrance. "… a little over three thousand dollars as well as the contents of her apartment. A list appended to the will identifies individuals who are to receive particular items, apparently of sentimental value."

Judy felt the blood drain from her face. This made no sense. It could not be true. Must not be true. She would wait for clarification. Yet Mr. Lloyd's words were clear.

He glanced at the sheet of paper lying beside the will. "You are included in the list of individuals to receive particular items. I find this puzzling, since anything not specifically excluded goes to you as a matter of course. Of course it was the late Mr. Wilson, not I, who drew up this will. He looked after your mother's legal affairs for many years and must have understood her wish to single out a quilt in this way. At any rate, here are your mother's exact words: 'I leave my quilt to my daughter, Judy Aylesworth, in the hope that she will finally appreciate its true value.'"

"Her quilt?" Judy's lips trembled. Was this Mom's idea of a joke?

Mr. Lloyd smiled in a kind, patient way. "Presumably you know the particular quilt she had in mind?"

"In her later years, she kept just one. Through her life, she made dozens of quilts. The others are long gone."

"Whatever her reason may have been, your mother's intention is clear." He looked again at the papers in front of him. "Well, that sums it up. Now the will goes to probate."

"Just a minute!" Judy pulled her thoughts together. "There's been a mistake. My mother put the two hundred and fifty thousand dollars from the sale of her house into Guaranteed Investment Certificates. I remember the discussion very well. We decided that she should buy GIC's in order to increase her income while keeping the capital safe."

Mr. Lloyd shook his head. "There are no GIC's. Your mother used the proceeds from the sale of her house to purchase a single-life annuity."

"I don't believe this." Judy sank back in the chair.

"It was a reasonable thing to do," Mr. Lloyd said mildly. "The annuity assured her of a more ample monthly income for the remainder of her life. Upon her death …" He lifted his shoulders in an eloquent shrug, "… the money died with her."

Judy felt suddenly sick, and at the same time weak with rage. After everything she had done for Mom! Driven her to appointments. Taken care of her shopping. Given up an afternoon every week to sit listening to stories about the good old days on the farm. And this was the thanks she received!

He broke in upon her thoughts. "Now we need your signature." He placed a bunch of papers in front of her. "Sign here, and here. These documents must be in triplicate."

In a daze, Judy signed the papers. She felt faint as Mr. Lloyd showed her from his office.

Driving home, Judy nearly slammed her elderly Chevette into an SUV stopped at a red light. After that, she forced herself to focus. Her hands clamped to the wheel, she drove like a robot.

How could any mother treat her daughter like that, reaching from beyond the grave to add insult to injury? Mom knew Judy hated that quilt. For years she had urged her mother to throw it away. It was morbid for an old woman to sit there fingering fabric squares, mumbling in her monotone, "This one came from your father's good suit. He bought it when they elected him reeve." She went on and on like that about every square.

Judy parked in the driveway and sat for several minutes with her head in her hands. Three thousand dollars wouldn't even pay for the coffin, let alone the other funeral home charges. How could she tell Wayne about this? He had urged her to select the "Just Cremation" option. But no. Judy had wanted to give her mother a proper send-off.

At least the reception would not cost them anything. The ladies of Saint Alban's Altar Guild were providing sandwiches, cupcakes, and tea. If they expected a legacy, they too were in for a surprise. The thought of their disappointment was Judy's only consolation.

Stepping from the car, Judy saw that Wayne had not mown the lawn. Typical. In May the grass grew so fast that most neighbours cut it every week. Not Wayne. In the five years since his business failed, he had stopped caring what people thought.

She could hear the television as soon as she opened the front door. Wayne was watching "The Price Is Right".

"You promised to cut the grass!" she yelled from the front hall.

He sat up with a start when she marched into the living room. "I was going to. Can't I sit down for five minutes without you jumping on me?"

The corduroy sofa cushion had left visible creases on the side of his face. On the coffee table in front of the sofa, beside the TV remote, were two empty Budweiser bottles and an empty potato-chip bag.

Judy picked up the remote and turned off the set. It crackled as the screen went blank.

"So what was in the will?" Wayne asked. "How much did she leave you?"

"Nothing. Or darn close."

"So she left the whole caboodle to Saint Alban's Church. I thought she might. After all we did for her!"

Judy could have asked Wayne what he had ever done for Mom, but she did not have enough energy for a fight.

"There was nothing to leave. My mother spent it all on a single-life annuity."

Without waiting for Wayne's response, she climbed the stairs, entered the bedroom, and threw herself upon the bed.

All her life she had knocked herself out trying to please Mom. But when had she ever received one word of praise or gratitude? When she was a teenager, it was all, "Tim did this," and "Tim did that." Of course she had resented it. Who wouldn't? Sometimes she had been jealous of Tim, but she had loved him all the same. Her heart broke, too, when he died.

After Tim's death, Dad grew silent, didn't want to talk about Tim. Mom didn't want to talk about anything else. It was, "Tim would have done this," and "Tim would have done that." Sometimes Judy had wanted to scream, "Oh, stop it! Look at me. You still have your daughter!"

Maybe she should have screamed. But it wouldn't have made any difference. Mom never appreciated anything she did. Even when she gave her that expensive mohair throw to replace the shabby old quilt, her mother kept on nagging, "Where's my quilt? Where have you put my quilt? You haven't put it in the wash, have you?"

In the wash! Putting it out with the garbage would have made more sense. But Judy had not done either. The quilt was in the basement, where it had been for the past two years, ever since she had sneaked it from her mother's apartment.

She would have thrown it out, had she not found a use for it as a dust cover. Wayne had inherited a tall china cabinet that would not fit in their poky little dining room. Judy had wanted to sell the china cabinet, but Wayne refused, even though they were short of money. So there it sat in the basement, with the quilt draped over it. With their house needing a new roof, they'd have to sell it now, whatever Wayne said.

Mom did not know that Judy had gone without winter boots to buy that mohair throw. Mom did not know that Aylesworth Hardware had closed its doors five years ago or that Judy and Wayne were forced to live on his Old Age Security, plus the Guaranteed Income Supplement that the government doled out. Judy never told her mother about any of that. Pride, mostly. Mom always said that Wayne had no "get up and go".

Not like Judy's father, who had plenty. In Mom's eyes, Township Reeve William Jessop was the greatest Canadian since Sir John A. Macdonald.

Maybe Wayne didn't have much get "up and go", but he had been a responsible businessman. The hardware store had provided a decent income until Home Depot moved into town. It wasn't Wayne's fault that he couldn't survive competition on that scale.

From outside came the roar of a gas-powered lawn mower. Wayne was cutting the grass. Well, that was a start. Judy rose from the bed and went downstairs. She picked up the beer bottles and the chip bag. Although the reception after the funeral would be in Saint Alban's Parish Hall, plenty of people would be dropping by the house. Neighbours bearing casseroles. The Altar Guild ladies clucking their condolences. The minister. Judy never attended church, but the Reverend Mr. Clerpool was not a man to give up easily.

Judy carried the empties down to the basement to replace them in the carton from The Beer Store. By the light of the forty-watt overhead bulb, the china cabinet, draped in the old quilt, looked like a dark and dusty ghost lurking in one corner. Before returning upstairs, Judy paused in front of it.

My Book of Memories. That's what her mother had called it. Each square brought back a memory. Tim's high school graduation. Dad's election as reeve. But not one square for anything Judy ever did. "I guess there weren't any old clothes of yours in the scrap bag," Mom had said when Judy pointed this out. "No need to take on about it." Judy knew that the omission had not been deliberate. That made it worse, in a way.

She pulled the quilt off the china cabinet and gave it a shake. I'll put it with the stuff from her apartment, she thought as she folded it. It might fetch a couple of dollars at auction. There are always a few crazies who go gaga over old things.

After the funeral, after the hugs and condolences, the chopped-egg sandwiches and the cupcakes, Judy had three days to remove from her mother's apartment the few things that she wanted to keep. There was a coffee table with carved legs, a set of Limoges china, and a Persian carpet. The rest, along with the quilt, she left for Ted Porter Auction Services to clear out.

"So that's that," she said to herself as she closed the door to her mother's apartment. Judy had no intention of attending the auction. She would never have to look at that quilt again.

Two weeks later, on the evening before the auction, Judy sat at the kitchen table looking over her mother's financial statements, adding up assets and liabilities. She was going over the figures a second time when she noticed something odd. A discrepancy. Her mother had realized two hundred and fifty thousand dollars from the sale of her house. Yet the purchase price of her single-life annuity had been precisely two hundred thousand.

Fifty thousand dollars were missing. Fifty thousand!

What had Mom done with that money?

She had not travelled. She had not bought a car. Her only extravagance was the luxury apartment, and Judy knew to the exact cent what the rent had been.

Fifty thousand dollars vanished without a trace.

She must have hidden it.

But where?

How many hiding places could there be in a one-bedroom apartment?

The answer took Judy's breath away. "I leave my quilt to my daughter, Judy Aylesworth, in the hope that she will finally appreciate its true value."

The Auction

Alice Wiltsie paused at the table that Ted Porter Auction Services had set up inside the entrance of the Lions Club Hall. She wrote her name, address and telephone number in the register, and then picked up a copy of the list of auction lots, as well as a wooden paddle with her bidding number.

The Lions Club Hall was a low, concrete-block building with a corrugated metal roof and no air conditioning. Even with the doors open and the two ceiling fans turning, the temperature was barely tolerable at nine forty-five on this June morning. Although Alice had dressed for the weather, wearing a sundress that exposed her winter-pale shoulders, she already felt sticky with perspiration.

Alice had come to the auction with one purpose: to bid on the seven Mennonite quilts that Porter Auction Services had advertised in yesterday's *Belleville Intelligencer*. She wanted those quilts for the seven guestrooms of her B & B, which would open in only five days. They would be the perfect finishing touch, she thought.

Scanning the crowded hall for her friend Selena, Alice spotted her in the second row of chairs facing the low stage. Next to her was an empty chair. Alice knew that Selena had saved it for her. Selena always arrived early at auction sales, and always saved her a seat.

Alice checked the big clock on the wall. Before the bidding began, Alice would have ten minutes to inspect the quilts. Steering around grandfather clocks, washstands, cradles, churns and pine blanket boxes, she made her way to the far wall, where the seven quilts were displayed, each on its own rack.

They were as good as the advertisement had promised. Impeccable workmanship. Each quilt was unique, yet they shared a common rustic charm. The one she liked most had a yellow butterfly appliquéd in one corner, its wings spread partly over the adjoining blue and green squares.

I'll go as high as six hundred dollars to get this one, Alice thought. *Four hundred tops for each of the others.*

Alice checked the list of auction lots. The quilts were in Lot #3. They would come up to auction early. That was lucky. In a couple of hours she could be home again, hanging pictures and looking after dozens of other details.

A series of loud clicks drew her attention to the stage. Ted Porter was tapping the microphone – his practice both to test it and to announce that the auction was about to begin. He was a swarthy, heavy-set man, dressed in his customary black suit with a white shirt open at the neck.

On her way to her seat, Alice noticed an eighth quilt. Not worthy of a display rack, it lay loosely folded on a table, sharing the space with heaps of towels and linens.

She stopped automatically – not that she needed an eighth quilt.

Unlike the beautiful Mennonite quilts, this one was shabby and plain. No pattern. Merely a patchwork of stitched-together squares, such as a frugal housewife of an earlier age would have salvaged from cast-off clothes. Alice briefly fingered the dark blue backing, which looked much newer than the worn squares. The backing must be a replacement, she thought as she turned away.

Squeezing past people's knees and around empty cartons brought to hold the treasures that would-be bidders hoped to carry home, she reached the unoccupied chair.

"Did you see the Mennonite quilts?" Selena asked when Alice had dropped into her seat.

"Yes. They're gorgeous."

"There's another quilt in Lot #2."

"I noticed that one. It's not much. Besides, I only need seven."

"Just thought I'd mention it. Lot #2 comes from the Jessop Estate."

"Who's Jessop?"

"You never heard of Reeve Jessop? Bill Jessop was a big man in local politics back in the 1970's, before you moved to Eastern Ontario. His widow died recently. She was nearly ninety."

"Hmm," Alice said, not paying much attention. Her eyes were on the auctioneer.

"Let's get moving, folks." Porter's voice boomed through the hall. "We got twenty lots to clear today."

Oil lamps came first, carried to an onstage table by Porter's assistants, a native girl in tight jeans and an androgynous youth with floppy blond hair.

These lamps were no homely farmhouse specimens, but ornate artifacts with fonts of amber or cranberry glass, some decorated with opalescent swirls. Selena's breathing was rapid as one by one the lamps fell to the auctioneer's hammer. But her paddle remained on her lap.

"I can't believe you didn't bid on any of those lamps," Alice said, "the way you go for old glass."

"George has put me on a budget. He'll murder me if I spend more than one hundred dollars at this sale. I'm saving myself for an 1880's covered compote." She sighed. "The finial is a tiny frosted-glass lion, ready to pounce. It's in Lot #20. Looks as if I'll be here all day."

"Are you likely to get an 1880's compote for one hundred dollars?"

"Not a chance. I'll have to pay twice that."

"What about the one-hundred-dollar limit?"

"I won't tell George. I brought cash. I'm safe so long as I lose the receipt."

Alice laughed. "Lies are the lubricant that keeps a marriage running smoothly."

"Lot #2 coming up," Porter announced.

"Shall I get us some iced tea?" Alice asked as the androgynous youth held up a gilt-framed portrait of a pre-Raphaelite lady with tragic eyes.

"Wait," Selena murmured. "The Jessop stuff is in this lot."

"That's okay. I'm just here for the quilts." Alice rose from her chair.

"Excuse me. Excuse me." She squeezed past people whose tense expressions betrayed their eagerness to witness the disposal of the Widow Jessop's furniture, china, linens and other possessions and made her way to the serving counter. Behind the counter, Lionesses dispensed coffee, cool drinks, hot dogs and homemade pie. Waiting in line, she watched the progress of the auction. Halfway through Lot #2, the old quilt came up. Porter's assistants each gripped a corner of the quilt and held it high.

"Now here's a piece of Eastern Ontario history," Porter announced. "A quilt from the home of Hay Bay's most famous citizen. Who'll start the bidding at fifty dollars?"

No response.

"Make it twenty-five," Porter suggested.

Silence.

"Don't sit on your hands! Gimme a bid! Any bid."

"Two bucks!" a man shouted. Laughter. A few groans.

Alice felt a pinch of sympathy for the poor, despised quilt. Somebody ought to bid. But not her. Whatever would she do with an eighth quilt, especially a worn old quilt like that?

Porter scowled. In a loud aside to his assistants, he barked, "Take it out of the sale."

They stepped from the stage, folded the quilt, and laid it on a cleared table.

"Lot #3 coming up," Porter announced.

Served at last, Alice paid for two cardboard cups of iced tea and carried them back to her place. She gulped down her tea quickly and then picked up her paddle, ready for action.

She had learned to identify the three types of people who attended country auction sales. Neighbours. Antiquers. Dealers. Neighbours came out of curiosity, voyeurs keen to inspect the possessions of people whom they knew or had known. Antiquers came because they were in the grip of the same addiction that Alice and Selena shared. As for dealers, they were a hard-boiled lot. Poker-faced, constantly scribbling in the margins of their lists, they were on the lookout for rare treasures to be picked up for a fraction of their true value.

Today Alice did not fear serious competition from neighbours, antiquers or dealers. The Mennonite quilts, which came from St. Jacobs, two hundred miles away, were neither local, nor antique, nor rare.

Porter's assistants removed the quilts from their racks and brought them up onto the stage. The butterfly quilt was first on the block.

"Let's get moving!" Porter urged. "Who'll start this at four hundred dollars?"

"Four hundred!" Alice raised her paddle. Sometimes it paid to be bold, to show other bidders they didn't have a chance.

"Do I hear five hundred?"

From behind Alice came a woman's voice. "Five hundred."

Alice turned to look. What she saw was money personified, a woman with sleek blond hair pushed back to reveal gold earrings set with gemstones that matched the apple-green of her silk blouse. Alice had never seen her before. Probably from Toronto, she thought.

"Six hundred." Alice held her breath.

"Seven."

Porter's eyes brightened.

"The bid is seven hundred dollars. Do I hear …?"

Porter's eyes met Alice's. She shook her head. She was out of her league. Game over.

"Going once at seven hundred dollars." A pause. "Going twice." Another pause. He was giving Alice time to reconsider.

If I don't get this quilt, there's no point in bidding on the others. It has to be seven quilts or no quilts. If it's no quilts, I've wasted half the morning sitting here. And what's a few hundred more, after the fortune we've already spent fixing up on the house?

"Eight hundred."

Admiration flashed in the auctioneer's eyes.

"Eight hundred is the bid. Do I hear nine hundred?"

He did not.

"Wow!" Selena whispered, *sotto voce.*

"Going once. Going twice. Going three times. Sold for eight hundred dollars."

Alice twisted in her seat to look around.

The blond's peach-tinted lower lip protruded in a pout that seemed to say she didn't want the damn quilt anyway.

Nor did she particularly want any of the other Mennonite quilts. There were other bidders, but none with Alice's determination. She swept the rest of the lot at four hundred each.

At the end of Lot #3, Porter announced, "Ten-minute break so I can go outside for a smoke." He switched off his mike.

Selena looked stunned. "You just spent three thousand, two hundred dollars."

"Who's counting?" Alice felt drunk with success. She stood up. "I'm leaving now. Those quilts were the only things I wanted."

"I'll help carry them to your car. Then I'm coming back."

As Alice made her way to the entrance, she noticed the blond inspecting a George III tall-case clock that was clearly the most valuable item in the sale. Her manicured fingers stroked the swan-neck pediment. That's what she is really after, Alice thought. The quilt with the butterfly had been no more than a passing whim.

With half the crowd lined up at the refreshment counter and the rest gone outside, Alice was the only person ready to settle her bill. She was writing a cheque at the table inside the entrance when Porter strolled up to her.

"You like quilts. You may as well take them all." He waved in the direction of the old quilt that lay abandoned on the table in front of the stage, and then he continued out the door.

"Why, thank you." Caught by surprise, Alice could not think what else to say. She might as well take it, she thought, since it was free.

"I'll get it for you," Selena said.

With four quilts piled in her arms, Alice could hardly see over the top as she went out the door, followed by Selena. The air was fresh outside the hall, and a light breeze stirred her hair.

They were putting the quilts on the back seat of Alice's car when suddenly an old Chevette with a defective muffler roared into the parking lot. Braking with a spray of gravel, it turned into the first space available.

"Somebody's in a big hurry," Selena commented as she closed the car door.

"Looks like it." Alice hugged Selena. "Good luck with the compote. See you later."

As Alice was fastening her seat belt, the driver of the Chevette got out. She was a stocky woman, late middle-age, wearing a pink ultra-suede pantsuit. She had short salt-and-pepper hair, and she wore pink button earrings the size of quarters. On her face was an expression of fierce determination. She slammed her car door and, arms pumping, ran toward the hall.

What's she's after? Alice wondered as the woman disappeared inside.

RIP

"You paid what for those quilts?"

"Twelve hundred dollars. And worth every penny." Alice prepared to brazen it out. Twelve hundred was an amount she could justify. If Gilbert knew that this figure was two thousand dollars short of the truth, he would have a stroke.

"Jesus!" Gilbert slumped forward on the settee, pressing the fingers of his left hand to his brow in a gesture that conveyed his effort to grasp the ungraspable. "We're in debt up to our eyeballs. Don't you get it?"

Alice picked up the copy of *Heritage Home* that was lying on a footstool and, making a show of tidying the room, placed it in the wicker basket that held magazines.

"Since we already owe the bank three hundred thousand, I don't see that an extra twelve hundred dollars makes much difference."

The Wiltses glared at each other. Gilbert was a retired high school math teacher, with thinning hair, a sallow complexion, and dark pouches under his eyes. In the game of stare-down, which Alice and Gilbert had been playing for thirty years, he was usually the winner.

"One of the quilts is for you," Alice said, making an effort to placate him. "And it didn't cost a cent."

"What the hell do you expect me to do with a quilt?"

She willed herself to sound pleasant. "You can spread it on the coach house floor to lie on while you work on the Morgan. It's an old quilt. The auctioneer threw it in because nobody wanted to bid on it." She forced a smile. "I'll show it to you."

Gilbert did not return her smile. One thing he had learned from thirty-five years teaching high school was the incompatibility of smiling with maintaining discipline. He made a dismissive gesture with his hand, but no other response.

Apparently thinking that silence gave assent, Alice escaped to the kitchen, where all eight quilts lay stacked on the big harvest table (a steal at eight hundred dollars, two years ago) that took up most of the room.

Returning with the Jessop quilt, she dropped it onto Gilbert's lap. He stared at it bleakly.

"Feel how thick the padding is," she urged.

Gilbert squeezed one edge between his thumb and forefinger. "Not bad," he grumbled.

"At least give it a try. You have time to work on the Morgan for a couple of hours."

"You don't have more chores for me to do?"

"No. You did such a super job putting up the sign that you deserve a break." She forced another smile. "Go out to the coach house and enjoy yourself."

He stood up. "I think I'll do that."

There was a slight relaxation of his frown as he left the house, the quilt over his arm. He felt a mild satisfaction, as if an issue had been settled in his favour.

On his back under the car, Gilbert had to admit that lying on a quilt was decidedly better than on oil-puddled concrete. He shouldn't have growled at Alice. She meant well. And he felt a twinge of guilt for having criticized her extravagance. After all, he had paid forty thousand for the Morgan, not the twenty thousand that he told her. They were seriously in debt.

The debt was the $300,000 mortgage they had taken out to purchase the old McLaughlin house for Alice's B & B. Gilbert was not sure how she had talked him into it. The perfectly adequate home they had lived in for thirty years was finally mortgage-free. If they were going to move, they would have been smarter to downsize rather than buy a Victorian mansion three times larger than the house in which they had raised three children.

When Alice had first come up with her idea for a B & B, he had told her that she was out of her mind. But she forced him to listen, and he grudgingly admitted that she had done her homework. In a weak moment, he agreed to take a look. Undeniably, the place was dirt-cheap for something of its size, located in Belleville's finest old neighbourhood. The slate roof was in excellent condition. Apart from needing new plumbing and a modern electrical service, the red brick house with its oak floors and high ceilings was in fine condition.

What Alice had proposed was feasible. There would be a ground-floor apartment for the two of them, and seven guest bedrooms on the second and third storeys. Alice was enchanted by the turret, which would become one of the guest rooms. But for Gilbert it was the coach house at the end of the driveway that had been irresistible. He had foreseen that if they bought the property, the coach house could be his haven.

At first, Gilbert had doubted that a B & B could make much money. But after checking on the Internet, he changed his mind. Travellers who did not care for the Holiday Inn appeared to be smitten by Victorian mansions with turrets. Besides that, Alice was an excellent cook. And when it came to interior décor, her taste was flawless. Above all, he knew through experience that when she set her mind to do something, she worked her butt off to do it right

She had wanted to call the B&B "Victoria's Bower", until Gilbert snorted that such a name would be more suitable for a brothel than a bed and breakfast. "The Maples" was his suggestion. This was appropriate, he had pointed out, since there were three enormous maples on the property, their roots snaking expensively into the sewer lines.

Gilbert and Alice had made the sign together – a very professional-looking sign, if he said so himself. He had cut it out from plywood, and she had done the painting. The sign was pale grey, oval in shape, with green maple leaves in a stencilled wreath around fancy lettering embellished with graceful curlicues.

That morning, while Alice was at the auction, Gilbert had hung the sign, suspending it by two wrought-iron hooks from a pair of four-by-fours that he had earlier sunk in concrete.

Hanging the sign was the final act of a transformation of a dream into reality. It was also Gilbert's final contribution to Alice's grand project. Henceforth, he hoped, the B & B would be her domain, and the coach house would be his.

There was nowhere he would rather spend his days, unless it could be on the open road in a Bugatti Type 35. He had seen one once, in an auto show at the CNE in Toronto. Just looking at it, he had felt the wind in his hair and heard the music of rubber meeting the road. But for him such a car could never be more than a dream.

Gilbert had worked his way up from a 1929 Ford Model A to this fine 1924 Morgan Aero. He had never worked on a three-wheeler before, had never driven one. This car was rare, and the challenge extraordinary. Lying on his back on the quilt, absorbed by the problems posed by the archaic transmission with its rather unusual dual-chain drives, Gilbert surrendered himself to total bliss. Everything he needed was right here: his hands, his tools, and this amazing automobile.

The double doors of the coach house stood open, admitting a breeze as well as light. A brief shower earlier in the afternoon had cooled the air. When he turned his head, he could see raindrops on the grass, sparkling in the sunshine.

Alice knew better than to interrupt him when he was working on a car. In this private paradise, he had made clear, there was to be no intrusion of feminine chatter. Thus Gilbert's soul, basking in a state of perfect contentment, was unprepared for the sound of two female voices approaching.

The one was Alice's light soprano, her tone upbeat yet soothing. The other, which he did not recognize, had a querulous, nagging tone that would have caused him to retreat even further under the car, if that had been possible.

"I'm telling you," whined the unfamiliar voice, "I don't know how that quilt found its way into the auction. My dear mother made it with her own two hands. I would not have parted with it for a thousand dollars."

"No problem." That was Alice. "We can work this out."

Now Gilbert saw two pairs of legs standing in the open doorway. The longer pair was Alice's – smooth, and remarkably shapely for a woman in her fifties. The other pair of legs was stumpy and clad in pink slacks.

"Gilbert, Honey, can you crawl out from under there for a minute?"

"Not right now. I'm working on the transmission, and I have everything just about ready to remove."

"Please. It's important."

He sighed loudly enough to let the women hear his annoyance as he wriggled from under the car and rose to his feet.

"This is Judy Aylesworth," Alice said, indicating the stocky, grey-haired woman standing beside her. Gilbert wiped his hands along the sides of his sweatpants, wondering whether to offer to shake hands, and then deciding against it. "That quilt you were lying on belonged to Mrs. Aylesworth's mother. It was put into the auction by mistake."

"Is that a fact?" Gilbert knew that his tone was surly.

"I didn't realize what had happened until yesterday evening," Mrs. Aylesworth said. "First thing this morning, I drove here from Kingston. It should have been a forty-minute drive. I expected to arrive at the auction hall by nine o'clock when the doors opened; then there would have been plenty of time to pull the quilt out of the sale. But the drive took two hours. A tractor-trailer had tipped over on the 401. I should have taken #2 Highway, but I thought the 401 would be faster."

"Usually is," Gilbert grunted.

"When I finally got there, the woman on the desk at the auction hall told me someone had bought the quilt, paid the bill and left just minutes before I arrived. She refused to give me a name or address, even though she had them on a sheet of paper right there in front of her. She said she had to get Mr. Porter's permission to identify a buyer. So I had to wait another hour before he broke for lunch and she asked him."

"Well, I didn't actually buy it ..." Alice's voice trailed off.

Gilbert was about to say, "You're welcome to take it," when he saw Alice shake her head a mere fraction of an inch. She had a glint in her eye.

"Gilbert, Mrs. Aylesworth has offered to pay us double what the quilt cost me."

"Oh?" He refrained from pointing out that two times zero was still zero. After clearing his throat, he said, "Mrs. Aylesworth, let's try a different approach. It would be better if you were to name the figure you have in mind."

Mrs. Aylesworth's gaze shifted to Alice's face, seeking help. Alice shrugged.

"Two hundred?" Mrs. Aylesworth placed one hand on the Morgan's fender, as if to steady herself.

"Hmm," said Gilbert. "Did I not hear you say that you wouldn't part with that quilt for one thousand dollars?"

"Just a way of speaking." An unsteady laugh.

"Well, Mrs. Aylesworth, Alice and I will talk it over this evening. Give us a call tomorrow and we'll tell you what we decide."

Alice jumped in. "Gilbert, two hundred is plenty. We can decide right now."

Gilbert shook his head. "Tomorrow. Now if you'll excuse me, I want to get back to what I was doing." He dropped to the coach house floor, rolled onto his back, and disappeared under the car.

"I'm so sorry," he heard Alice say as the women walked away. "I can't imagine what's gotten into him. Your offer is more than fair. Come back tomorrow morning. I'm sure I can convince him."

"Well, it's certainly putting me to a lot of extra trouble."

"That's men, isn't it?"

A minute later, he heard a car with a defective muffler drive away.

In ten seconds, Alice returned.

"Are you crazy? What if she doesn't come back?"

"She will," he grunted as he crawled out again. "Look, she wouldn't have offered two hundred if there weren't a catch somewhere." He dragged the quilt from under the car and rolled it into a bundle. "Let's have a look."

It took Alice two hours to pick out the stitching, ten to put the quilt back together again. By the time she had finished, her eyes stung with fatigue. Still, fifty thousand dollars was good pay for twelve hours' work.

Mrs. Aylesworth returned in the morning. She was smiling as she counted out two hundred dollars.

Gilbert was smiling, too.

What about that Bugatti? Or maybe a Duesenberg J. It looked as if the Wiltses' luck was beginning to turn. Might as well dream big, if you're going to dream at all.

Acknowledgements

Thanks to Maureen Whyte, publisher of Seraphim Editions, for her unflagging faith and determination; to my daughter Alison Baxter Lean for her generous criticism throughout the writing of these stories; to my circle of first readers, Debbie Welland, Alexandra Gall, Linda Helson, Barbara Ledger, and Trudi Down of the Creative Writing Group, Canadian Federation of University Women (Hamilton Branch); to Anne Haberl, Janet Myers and Chris Pannell for their insightful comments on particular stories; to Gordon King for his expertise on the subject of classic cars; to George Down for his meticulous editing.

Thanks to the editors of the following magazines and anthologies where some of these stories first appeared: *Hammered Out, Ellery Queen's Mystery Magazine, Indian Country Noir, Going Out with a Bang.*

"The Quilt", the opening story in the "Patchwork Pieces" quartet, was included in *A Twist of Malice,* Jean Rae Baxter's first short story collection (Seraphim Editions, 2005).

"After Annabelle" received the 2010 John Kenneth Galbraith Literary Award.

The following stories were shortlisted for awards: "The Errand", Surrey International Writers' Conference, 2010; "Devotion", John Kenneth Galbraith Literary Award, 2010; "Hilda Perly", John Kenneth Galbraith Literary Award, 2009; "Travelling by the Grand Bus Line", Silver Hammer Award, 2007.